THE EMBRACE OF LIGHT AND DARKNESS

THE EMBRACE OF LIGHT AND DARKNESS

A PENTALOGY

[Dance of Sounds. The Matter of Matter, The Home of the World,
All Women in One, The Light of the Mind]

DEJAN STOJANOVIĆ

New Avenue Books

THE EMBRACE OF LIGHT AND DARKNESS
A PENTALOGY
[Dance of Sounds. The Matter of Matter, The Home of the World, All Women
in One, The Light of the Mind]

Copyright © 2025 New Avenue Books

The Embrace of Light and Darkness is a pentalogy comprising five poetry collections written in English between 2005 and 2010, with a few exceptions that were added or corrected later. The individual books within this pentalogy are titled: *Dance of Sounds, The Matter of Matter, The Home of the World, All Women in One,* and *The Light of the Mind.*

New Avenue Books

First Edition in English

Library of Congress Control Number: 2025934962

ISBN-13: 978-1-966571-16-2

NOTE TO THIS EDITION

The Embrace of Light and Darkness is a pentalogy comprising five books of poetry written in English between 2005 and 2010, with a few exceptions that were added or corrected later. The individual books within this pentalogy are titled: *Dance of Sounds, The Matter of Matter, The Home of the World, All Women in One,* and *The Light of the Mind.*

Contents

DANCE OF SOUNDS

FORGOTTEN HOME

FORGOTTEN HOME

My feelings are too loud for words
And too shy for the world.
See the Light and have a dream
In your hidden garden.
No need for words.

The words are but shadows
Of stories never told,
Shining from distant kingdoms,
Reminding you of a forgotten home.

Light rays will tell you the story.
There is another alphabet
Whispering from every leaf,
Singing from every river,
Shimmering from every sky.

BEING LATE

The simplicity and ease of movement
Of heavenly bodies stem from precision.
The Sun is never late to rise upon the Earth,
The Moon is never late to cause the tides,
The Earth is never late to greet the Sun and the Moon.
Thus, accidents are not accidents,
But precise arrivals at the wrong-right time.
Love is seldom simple.
Too often, feelings arrive too soon,
Waiting for thoughts that often come too late.
I, too, wanted to be simple and precise,
Like the Sun, the Moon, and the Earth,
But the Earth has been booked billions of years in advance,
Designed to meet all desires, all arrivals,
All sunrises, all sunsets, and all departures,
So I will have to be a little bit late.

TASK OF A POET

To hear never-heard sounds,
To see never-seen colors and shapes,
To try to understand the imperceptible
Power pervading the world;
To fly and find pure, ethereal substances
Beyond material form,
Yet part of the invisible essence that infuses reality.
To hear the soul of another and whisper to them;
To be a lantern in the darkness
Or an umbrella on a stormy day;
To feel much more deeply than to know.
To be the eyes of an eagle, the slope of a mountain;
To be a wave attuned to the pull of the Moon;
To be a tree that remembers the stories of its leaves;
To be an unnoticed pedestrian on the streets
Of bustling cities, observing and reflecting.
To be a smile on a woman's face
And shine in her memory
As a moment saved without planning.

SOUNDS OF IMAGINATION

I imagined I was a mountain,
Then I became a cloud over that mountain.
Lightning and thunder pummeled the mountain,
Pierced the heart of the Earth,
Becoming lava and exploding as a volcano.

I imagined I was a star,
Light traveling into space.
Then I grew as a tree,
With leaves of galaxies eating the light,
Becoming the angel of life and the bearer of light.

I imagined I was a black hole,
Flying through myself and swallowing myself,
While eating others to consume the abyss of energy.
But still, holding the whole galaxy in order,
Keeping billions of stars circling me.

I imagined I was God for a millisecond
And became speechless for a long time.

BIG MINIATURE

To transform a grimace into a sound
Sounds impossible, yet it is possible
To transform a vision into music,
Breaking free from an enslaved personality
To become impersonal by transforming
Into sand, water, or light,
To feel the air and breathe it in
By becoming the air, a bird,
The first cell, the first man,
A wandering comet, a dying star,
A newborn cluster of stars
And hear the melody of galaxies,
Experience the Love of black stars,
The hellish or heavenly nature of quasars,
Be in everything and come back
To a minuscule particle of personality
To discover how magnificent all of this is.

DANCING OF SOUNDS

There is a moonlight note
In the *Moonlight Sonata;*
There is a thunderous note
In an angry sky.

Sound, unbound by nature,
Is confined by art.
There is no competition between
A nightingale and a violin.

Nature rewards and punishes
In unpredictable ways;
Art is apotheosis;
Often, the complaint of beauty.

Nature is an outcry,
Unpolished truth;
The art—a euphemism—
Tamed wilderness.

SILENCE IS THE UNIVERSAL LIBRARY

Is there ever a true moment of silence?
Such a moment cannot exist
Unless we return
To the world before its creation.

Since nothing is absolute
There is no absolute silence—
Only the appearance
Of temporary peace.

Since real silence does not exist,
Silence encompasses all sounds,
All words, all languages,
All knowledge, and all memory.

Everything is contained within this library
In the Brain of the Universe—
Its source of inexhaustible energy,
The Library of Silence.

POSSIBILITY

Everything may seem impossible
Yet everything can also appear possible.
Possible impossibilities arise
From seemingly impossible possibilities,
Or perhaps impossible possibilities
Blossom from the impossibly possible.

A possibility is largely a matter of attitude,
A choice to select
From the realm of impossible options,
When one promising opportunity
Turns into a viable solution.

UNDERSTANDING

Is it possible to understand the impossible?

Based on the law of probability,
Everything is possible
Because the sheer existence of possibility
Confirms the existence of impossibility.
To understand the possible
Means to grasp the impossible.

SIMPLICITY

The most complicated skill
Is to be simple.

To say more while saying less
Is the secret of being simple.

To not say all that can be said
Is the secret of discipline and economy.

To leave out beautiful sunsets
Is the secret of good taste.

To hide feelings when you are near crying
Is the secret of dignity.

To cut and tighten sentences
Is the secret of mastery.

To keep the air fresh among words
Is the secret of verbal cleanliness.

To write good poems
Is the secret of brevity.

To go against the grain
Is the secret of bravery.

To risk life to save a smile on the face of a woman or a child
Is the secret of chivalry.

To go where no one else has ever gone before
Is the secret of heroism.

To expect to be kissed having bad breath
Is the secret of a fool.

Words rich in meaning
Can be cheap in sound effects.

QUIVER OF EMOTION

The quiver transforms the sound into music.
A feather caressing the mind,
Enters the bloodstream as feelings grow,
Becoming a current of emotions
That transform the soul into a celestial ship,
Carried by the current.
What begins as a quiver becomes a river;
The river becomes the ocean,
The ocean becomes an emotion,
And you feel it.

FORGOTTEN SOUNDS

GHAZAL OF LOVE

I cherish the fresh sounds of love;
Only the new can heal an old love.

As I watch the waves embrace the shore,
I long to be a wave of love.

In quarrels, there is no true hatred,
Only folly and a lack of love.

The sun shines upon me,
And I reflect that light upon the world with love.

I journey through my memories
To discover newfound love.

Sing to me, sea; sing to me, sky,
And let the world unfold from love.

A MAN WITH A GUITAR

Men talk in the public square,

Pigeons eat on the sidewalk and fly,

Women flirt and feed the pigeons.

Men, envious of pigeons,

Desire more attention from the women

But women only notice birds who know how to sing.

A nightingale starts singing

And attention moves from pigeons to nightingales;

There comes a man with a guitar, and he starts playing

And singing like a nightingale.

A woman allured by these new sounds

Forgets the pigeons and nightingales;

She shyly starts to sing

And turns to a man with a guitar.

THE BOOK OF BOOKS

An aspiring poet is usually advised
To use dictionaries, encyclopedias,
Grammar books, books of style, dictionary of rhyme,
Books on how to write and attendance at workshops.

To write, do write. But what about creativity?
How do you learn creativity? How to make sounds
Make love in the soul so one can continue
Making love with the page? How to

Learn from books that go unnoticed,
Gather glances, faces, metamorphoses
Of sounds, lives, territories, languages,
From a huge treasury of hidden sounds,

Hidden meanings flying in our faces unrecognized?
There is no grammar book to explain the world,
There is no book of style to explain the grace
Of a moonlight over the waves telling stories

To fishermen that learned from the sea;
To sailors, warriors that learned from losses and wins;
To birds that fly without support yet sing

Fed by notes from the biggest treasury

Of sounds, meanings, styles, dictionaries,

Histories, tragedies, deaths, births, revivals.

Yet this book is the place to start

And the place to go to for advice.

SERIOUS BUSINESS

If I were to share my struggles,
You might find it unsettling and discomforting
But there's no reason for that;
By sharing, we can start to recognize
The importance of simple beauty,
Which often goes ignored.

Busy with the expensive success,
We forget the free beauty—
Lying sad just around the corner,
Only an instant away,
Unnoticed and wasted.

SADNESS AND HAPPINESS

I cannot express everything I truly want to say,
And that makes me sad.

I cannot see all that I wish to see,
And that makes me sad.

I cannot visit even the closest neighbors in the Universe,
And that makes me sad.

I cannot read all that I want to read,
And that makes me sad.

I cannot love as much as I desire,
And that makes me sad.

I cannot be loved as much as I wish to be,
And that makes me sad.

But I have lived,
And for that, I am happy.

WISHFUL THINKING

"I wish I could sing like you,"
Said the frog to the nightingale.
"I would also like to have wings
So that I could fly while I sing,
Instead of having to jump from pond to pond."

"Caw, caw!" chirped the nightingale
As it flew away.

FERTILE GROUND

If raindrops

    D

    R

    O

    P

Into the right ears

    M

    U

    S

     I

    C

Starts growing from fertile ground

FORGOTTEN SOUNDS

No more messages,
No more instructions.
Stop!
Motors of progress,
Engines of alienation.

Forget
Big words and slogans,
Proclamations and declarations.

Wake up
To the forgotten sounds,
Sincere music.

Move
In a new direction,
From that very place.

Rediscover
The old melody
Of a sleepy world within you.
Then go,
Aiming as far as possible,
And never look back.

THE OLD SOUND

I am tired of all the new sounds;
They insult my sense of hearing.

I am weary of the countless variations of the same notes,
With this cacophony rearranged into new rhythms.

I can't hear anything anymore;
I feel like I am becoming deaf.

In a world filled with so many sounds,
I struggle to recognize any of them.

It's just a sea of noise—
Waves of sounds crashing monotonously.

Swimming in this ocean of indistinct noises,
I am unable to hear anything that brings me recognition.

I am frustrated and angry.

FORGOTTEN SERENADES

SERENADE

I enjoy serenading you,
Though I never admit it.
I serenade you when you can't hear anything
And while you are asleep.

I serenade you as you wake,
Never forgetting your preferences:
When you like it, and how you like it.
You enjoy waking up to calla lilies,

Along with my melodies,
And my plans for the new day,
You can hear the music when I invite you
To the park for lunch on a blanket.

You appreciate that I admire your jeans
As much as your gowns.
You enjoy that I understand you like
Grass as much as marble floors.

You cherish the sound of each morning
That brings new opportunities.
You value all the unseen gifts
That visually inspire you every day.

YOU ARE WHAT YOU SEE

They say *you are what you think*,
And they are right.
Your thoughts are shaped by what you see,
And they reflect your perceptions.

When you see the Light, you become the Light,
You transform into water that nurtures a flower,
A fountain flowing back into itself,
Opening up the entire Universe.

You perceive what you think,
And you become what you envision.
In the depths of your mind
You can foresee the Light ahead in the Darkness.

Your vision is your Light
Awakening you to the forgotten sound
Of the healer that sleeps within you.
That inner healer is your only Savior.

THE DRAMA OF LOVE AND HATE

Love and hate are driven by passion.
Both emotions originate from the heart
Entering our lives without much reasoning.
They can seem irrational, even dangerous—
Two opposing forces in the human experience.

The result is that hearts that harbor hate
Eventually corrode and lead to self-destruction,
While hearts that nourish love
Remain bright and serene,
Regardless of the circumstances.

There is hardly any remedy
For either a loving heart or a hating one.

A MAN AND HIS SHADOW

He walks down the street,
Followed by his shadow
As his only companion.
He asks the shadow for direction
Toward something new—
A new city, a new street,
A new life, new feelings.
He longs to escape his own skin
And follow a new shadow
Toward a new man,
New skin, new life.

"That is impossible,
I will always follow only you,"
The shadow replies.

END OF THE LABYRINTH

He tries to find the exit
Within himself,
But there is no door.

He walks
Through the inner labyrinth
To deceive his desires.

Perhaps there is an entrance
At the end of the labyrinth,
But there is no end.

MY OTHER SELF

I am a slave to desire,
I am a slave to pride,
I am a slave to vice,
I am a slave to success.

"Get rid of desire," desire said.
"Get rid of pride," pride said.
"Get rid of vices," honor said.
"Get rid of competition," success said.

I will still be a slave to sin,
A slave to materialism,
A slave to love,
A slave to myself.

"Get rid of sin and lust,
Of materialism and love,
And you will get rid of yourself,"
Said my other self.

"Are you proposing suicide?" I asked sadly.
"No, I would never suggest that," my other self replied.
"Then what are you trying to say?"
"Just be yourself," said my other self.

MY LIFE

My life made choices for me,
And many of them were poor;
My life endured hardships on my behalf,
And I felt their weight.

My life was both carefree and strict;
I was its disciple.
My life embraced joy for me,
And I felt it within.

This could easily become a very long list,
One that may never end;
I must cut it short,
And my life senses it.

THE LAND BEYOND

There is a land beyond our land,
There is life beyond our lives,
There is a world we do not see.
It seems to be beyond far
Because it's far within and near.

The world beyond and the world here,
Both worlds are far and near.
The farthest land is also the closest.
It's not a matter of time and space,
It is a matter of sense and attitude—

To know how to stay in yet fly far,
To understand how to stay outside
When moving far in what is near.

KNOWLEDGE

If we had true insight,
We would be terrified.
We could see nothing,
Yet perceive everything and nothing at once.

Our senses highlight our limitations.
They expand our vision within certain boundaries
And enhance our understanding through pleasure.
Without pleasure, there is no sight nor measure.

Complete knowledge leads to the annihilation
Of the desire to see, touch, or feel.
The world is experienced only through our senses
And remains untouched by knowledge alone, without feeling.

OLD AND NEW

If an ancient man had seen planes two thousand years ago
He would have thought they were birds
Or angels from another world
Or messengers from other planets.

Every new machine would have surprised him—
The car, the TV, the radio, the phone, the camera.
He might have believed he was a savage
Who didn't understand these marvels.

If he had seen a computer
And observed people talking on the Internet,
He would have thought it was a civilization
Much more advanced than his own.

After spending time among these messengers,
He would have learned that every child possessed
Knowledge and understanding of these technologies,
And knew how to use them.

Yet, after a while, he would have noticed
That none of them were advanced enough
To be considered wiser than the one
Who stated, "I know nothing."

PEOPLE

Some people complain there are too many people on earth,
Some people complain about secret societies,
Some people accuse others of not being able to wake up early,
Almost all people complain about something.

No people get rid of themselves to solve problem No.1,
No people disclose their agendas to solve problem No.2,
No people learn how to discipline themselves to solve problem
    No.3,
All people are enslaved by something.

FAITH

From dust to dust,
From ashes to ashes.
Is that all there is?

DICTIONARY OF SOUNDS

DICTIONARY OF SOUNDS

Born from the natural attraction
Of vowels and consonants
Alliterating or merging into a fugue

Of sounds flowing
From the fountain of language.
Meanings embodied

In blasts of thunder, chirping, blowing;
Sounds becoming meanings
In, for, and of themselves;

A huge dictionary of sounds
Craving to be recognized and translated
Either into language or into understanding.

ECHO

When you hear an idea
Lying between the sounds and the letters,
You uncover its meaning.

A sound flows silently
In the Universe, waiting
To be discovered in the obvious.

The Universe smiles,
Or you may find an omen
In a hostile land of the unknown.

Dig deeper and work harder;
Grow in the opposite direction
To see what lies beneath.

This effort nourishes the surface of sounds,
Allowing you to witness their creation
And hear their echoes on the way back home.

SOUND BOMBS

Everything in nature exists
Based on the law of attraction.
Lovemaking derives from that law,
Fighting comes from the friction of conquest.

We can be scared by sounds
Or seduced by sounds;
Sounds can kill us
Or reach heavenly heights.

Nobody has yet conceived a Sound Bomb—
Stronger than nuclear or neutron bombs.
It would be a fantastic bomb.
It could be the first bomb tested in outer space;

It could be sent far to distract
The future asteroid ready to strike the Earth;
It could be sent as a signal
To other civilizations throughout the Universe.

We should be careful with sound ideas,
For anyone may exploit them
And split the planet in half
While testing some new Sound.

EMISSARIES

Timeo Danaos et dona ferentes

They will come again with offerings,
Smiling as they always do
When planning a major attack
Late at night.

Be aware of the high notes,
Blissful faces, and their soft messages.
Listen for the silent sound
Of a finely wrapped gift.

PARADISE

Noise is needed for attention,
Flashy disposable sounds
Flushed after one use

To seduce and amuse sleepy spirits
With another sound, another appearance
Of an elevated spirit waiting

To come out into the big world
Ready for a new spectacle
A new Genie from a bottle

Of dreams sold in big boxes
Waving from the shelves,
Waving from billboards,

From the TV and the radio waves
Ready to come out,
Inviting us into a paradise
Decorated with Hell.

TODAY AND TOMORROW

There is always tomorrow,
Sounds of hope smiling from the distance
Alluring, drawing us into unknown territory;

There is always hope
We will arrive safely into the future,
Experience an unavoidable arrival of time waiting;

There is always time on hold,
To cut the future waiting
For those in the present time;

There is also sorrow
That doesn't wait for tomorrow.

TWO SOUNDS TALKING

Silence: I am a silent sound.
Sound: I am a sound sound.

Sound: Can I hear you if you are silent?
Silence: Yes you can, if you listen to me.

Sound: How can I listen to you if you are silent?
Silence: That is the whole point.

Sound: What is the whole point?
Silence: To learn how to listen to me.

Sound: If I learn, will I really hear you?
Silence: Yes, you will.

Sound: And you will sound like a sound?
Silence: I will sound like thunder.

Sound: That is nonsense—I am thunder.
Silence: Yes, a thunder of silence.

Silence: Who have you been talking to all this time?
Sound: You.

Silence: Who else could hear you without me?

Sound: Nobody.

Silence: There can be no sound without silence.

I am the Mother of all sounds.

Sound: You're right, Mother. You gave us life

And we all return to you either in quiet or with thunder.

SOUNDS OF LIFE AND LOVE

Love: Which is more important: Love or life?
Life: Without life, there would be no love.

Love: But without love, life would have no meaning.
Life: True, but life gives birth to love.

Love: And what gives rise to life?
Life: Life generates itself.

Love: Nothing can give birth to itself automatically,
There must be some cause, reason, or action.

Life: Life exists without any cause.
Love: If life is without a cause, then it lacks purpose.

Life: The purpose of life is to live.
Love: No, the purpose of life is love.

Life: You must be born to exist.
Without life, there is nothing.

Love: Life is nothing unless it comes from an inherent love.
You just don't understand.

SOUNDS OF LOVE AND HATE

Shall I say I love you? says Love.

No, you shall not.

Love loses its magic when declared.

Also, you would not be Love if you did not love me,

Says Hate.

Shall I say I hate you? says Hate.

No, you shall not.

I already know you hate me.

You would not be hate if you didn't hate me,

Says Love.

But if I said I hate you, what would you do? asks Love.

I would not believe you, says Hate.

Then I must kill you, says Love.

Then, you will be lonely, says Hate

And you will not be Love anymore.

You would kill yourself and become me.

FUTURE MAN

Perhaps you will laugh at me now,

But I forgive you.

I am already laughing

Along with you.

BEAUTY NEVER DIES

INVISIBLE TEACHER

You guide us on what to do,
Yet you often abandon us in critical moments,
Leaving us to fight alone.

You help us learn to walk,
But in times of isolation,
You leave us to rely on ourselves.

We stumble over obstacles
And though you are a teacher,
You are never a source of immediate help.

You are rarely warm enough—almost indifferent—
As you watch shipwrecks and broken homes,
Always unflinching.

You teach us in advance,
But remain silent when we need you most.
Your whereabouts are always unknown to us.

THE MOST IMPORTANT THINGS

The most important things are often unspoken—
Meaningful truths that surround us.
Unmerited treasures greet us at every turn—
Beauty unseen, waiting for a curious gaze,
Not too busy to notice the obvious.

You travel and breathe deeply,
Speechless yet aware of the unexpressed.
You search for the key to significant words,
And for a long time, you wait alone
To hear them emerge from the silence.

BEAUTY NEVER DIES

Singers may pass, but a song never dies,
Feeding the eternal flame.

New minds ignite,
Eager eyes yearn to listen, kindling passion.

Beauty recognizes the spark,
Shyly seducing from afar.

Beauty nurtures the flame,
Eyes cherish the beauty.

The source of fire—an omnipotent eye—
Hearing with eyes, seeing with ears.

THE LIFE OF WORDS

Some words fade away from too much freedom,
While others exist under oppression.
Some words expand in meaning,
While others merely reproduce.

Words that flourish through expression survive
And gain value and freedom,
But those that are forcefully multiplied
Diminish in worth, consumed by other words.

A FIFTY-FIFTY GAME

Suddenly, everything changed,
And nothing seemed as clear anymore—
At least, that's how it felt.

We don't know whom to blame now:
Deceiving eyes and misleading knowledge
Or God and a world guilty of trickery?

Are we betting on what our eyes see,
Or on what the world conceals?
It seems to be a fifty-fifty game.

APPEARANCES

We believed we had unraveled the mystery,
Convinced we understood the world,
Yet, nothing is more powerful than change,
Nothing is more healing or sobering,
Nothing else opens our eyes wider,
Making everything seem different.

A MORE IMPORTANT WORLD

There is a deeper world within you,
Waiting to be discovered—
Something profound yet unseen.
You can sense it on the sandy beach
As you listen to the tireless waves;
You hear a forgotten story.
Or, when lying on the grass,
You become one with the soil.
You can feel it beneath the oak tree
As you follow its shadow,
More precise than a Swiss watch,
You hear the clock inside you,
Suddenly awakening you.

SELF-RESPECT

Wherever you go,
You will always be yourself.

You may feel the urge to run away quickly:
That's how we learn to forget.

This strategy involves keeping yourself busy
And making it part of your daily routine.

It may be effective if your goal is to forget,
But if you wish to confront your feelings,
You must face them directly.

OBLIVION

To be born, to be young, to grow old, and to die—
To burn, to fly, to scream, to love, to live, and to die for life.

Without the ability to walk and feel tired,
What would you be?

But without understanding, why go through all of this—
Are you, or are you not?

What would you do to forget if, by chance,
You found what you were searching for?

What would you do, and would you regret
Ever asking the question, "Why?"

Eternal peace will handle everything,
And you will fall into oblivion without being asked.

LIFE AND TIME

Life and time are inseparable.

Without one, there is no other.

The vigor of life tells the story of time.

Time is a human construct—

A broken clock.

THE MATTER OF MATTER

BRAIN-UNIVERSE

SPIDER

The day justifies itself through the memories it promises.

Roses hold the secret of a scent unknown to them.

Lovers are often happy captives of sad illusions.

Children long for knowledge and beauty

That may not seem so lovely once discovered.

Nothing will be lost, but nothing will be saved either.

The future is as real as the past, yet the present does not exist.

Memory without a touch of sorrow is like food without spices.

The mind is both a hunter and the hunted.

There is no punishment because there is no true death.

We are enslaved more by our illusions than by our desires.

It is not the human being, but their mind stumbles over a rock.

The tireless spider weaves countless traps,

But the ultimate victim of its net is the spider itself.

SHAKESPEARE'S SOUL

Lightening thoughts shine in visions,

About life and everything under the stars.

Dreams that others do not dare to dream,

Streaming directly from the Source of Light,

Feed the soul nurtured by the natural rhythm of the heart

That hardly any computing algorithm can match.

Machines can organize words into sentences,

 Yet they do not have emotions that can create true art.

Even though machines can outsmart people in computing,

They do not possess the refinement of the human soul to be creative

But under the lead of humans and their creative nature

No height or goal is unachievable.

Machines can outsmart the human brain in many areas

But only human hearts can create true art.

BRAIN-UNIVERSE

The entire World exists within the human brain.
With 89 billion neurons and 100 trillion connections
Between them, along with 30 trillion cells in the human body,
Each one of us holds the Universe within.

Explore the vast interstellar regions of your imagination.

Thoughts are messages traveling between neuro-galaxies.
We are both the marvel of the Universe and the Universe itself.
Our thoughts and feelings shape the World we perceive
As well as the World that exists beyond our senses.

Recognize the wonders and answers you discover within.

A challenge arising from profound truths
Often goes unnoticed, even after we find an answer,
Yet, even without the answers, we believe that the ultimate
    secret
Lies in primordial nothingness filled with divine potential.

Your intuition will lead you more wisely than any textbook.

Cherish the miracle of being alive,

And the even more remarkable miracle of universal existence.
Embrace the wellspring of your imagination,
The force that unites the entire world.

Take a moment to look up and talk to the stars.

RESCUING HIDDEN THOUGHTS

Unlock the thoughts that lie dormant within words,
With art that brings life to ideas.

Uncover the hidden gems that await
In unexplored territories beyond language.

Embrace the adventure and discover
The miraculous worlds that reside within!

It's not you who is adrift;
It's your thoughts that feel isolated.

Invisible truths quietly illuminate
The minds willing to perceive the unseen.

Like the forces that support the Universe,
Profound thoughts patiently wait

For a brave explorer with the courage to dive
Into the wilderness and reveal their essence.

WORDS AND THOUGHTS

We need either a new language
Or a fresh way of thinking.
We have grown tired of empty words.

The problem lies not in the words themselves
Or in our experience, but in the speed
At which we reproduce them,
Compounded by deception.

Avoid using gimmicks to attract
New readers, clients, voters, or customers;
Refrain from relying on effects and showmanship;
Remove the "Sale" sign from words.

One authentic idea is worth more
Than an entire book filled with well-worn,
Stale knowledge and information.

THE MAGIC KEY

Some people navigate the world with confidence,
Yet they can get lost in a forest of thoughts.

Others may wander through life,
But find stability through their mental strength.

Some possess keys for many doors,
Yet they often end up in unwelcoming places.

Others never misplace their keys
But still feel lost in their experiences.

Some frequently lose their keys,
Yet navigate life with unwavering certainty.

Meanwhile, others don't need any magical keys
To explore the world and the rich depths of their souls.

LITTLE FAMILY

The World grew from a small dream,
Which blossomed into a massive tree,
With roots deeply anchored in the original dream,
Sustaining itself with the knowledge gained from it.

From a small dream, great hope emerges,
Spreading its roots across the sky,
Nourished by the wisdom acquired through dreaming.
A little family of dreamers shares the common vision.

Knowledge is less important than the life
Of a dream that supports those
In pursuit of forgotten truths.
A small family deciphers the ancient dream.

The sole purpose of the knowledge
From the original small dream is to nourish
The family of dreamers who long to uncover it.
Those who dream of knowledge embody knowledge itself.

In life, two dreams converge;
The knowledge of one becomes the essence of the other,
Yet, the dream remains unified.

Both sides are equally ineffective without each other.

One needs more knowledge to unravel the secret,
Yet knowledge is lifeless without the dream.

THE TRUTH INVISIBLY SHINES

The truth shines invisibly through silent sounds.
Help wisdom find you.

Don't go anywhere unless it is your own decision.
Be cautious of free advice.

Do not cling to unverified truths;
They are often less reliable than dreams.

Don't waste time complaining when faced with challenges—
A little more effort is all you need.

When you feel pressured from all sides,
Be determined enough to persevere

In order to reach the place you have always been,
Even if you weren't aware of it.

Freedom is not a matter of chance,
It is a matter of merit.

LONELY STONE

It is unwise to hoard all the knowledge you have acquired;
It is far more rewarding to uncover
Fragments of an immense treasure—
Joyful, tempting, challenging and fleeting.

The World is a solitary stone in limitless space.
Life flows like a river—
Meandering through existence
With knowledge as its only companion.

Understanding is akin to a solitary stone;
It is knowledge personified.
You are the witness, and you, too,
Are the knowledge, the river, and the stone.

ELOQUENT PSYCHOPATH

There is a new creature in the jungle—

An eloquent monkey.

He has lost much of his hair,

And appears slick and polished,

Dressed in expensive suits,

He always smiles, revealing his bright white teeth,

He enjoys reading, especially dictionaries;

He is charming and seductive,

Plays golf, and attends important events,

Mingling with many influential people.

You can spot him wherever cameras are present.

He makes promises, both possible and impossible,

He wakes up early because his schedule is always full.

His admirers often become his first victims,

Yet nobody realizes that he is

A new and dangerous creature in the jungle.

FREEDOM

One more discovery, and everything will be resolved.
But what should we do with all this freedom
If the secret lies only in a new patent
From an accountant turned scientist?
This expert understands the intricacies of the stock market,
Currency exchange, money supply,
The Federal Reserve, debts, mortgages,
Sub-mortgages, financing, and emerging trends.

This accountant-turned-scientist
Has now become known as a sophisticated investor;
His concern is for the well-being of free individuals
And the nations he proudly guides
Toward a state of absolute freedom for all.

This speculator labeled a sophisticated investor,
Pretends to lack knowledge—not about freedom
Or inventions, but about the illusion he creates.
He offers a lifeline to all who do not know
What to do with their newfound freedom.

THE MUSEUM OF WAX FIGURES

THE MUSEUM OF WAX FIGURES

He told us he would build a new society,
And then he left.
Another came
Promising to rebuild the old society,
But he, too, departed.

One followed after him,
And yet another,
Each making grand promises
To rectify past mistakes,
Only to leave as well.

The entire gallery of figures
Fills the Museum of Wax Faces,
Staring at us with the truth,
While we are left to manage the work
That remains after they have gone.

POETRY AND REALITY

Poetry is a translation of silent conversations
We have with the World,
Conveying emotions that transcend
What language can truly express.
It captures the essence of dreams
And the truths hidden within them.
Poetry is a beautiful illusion
That is larger than reality.
It serves as a meeting place for souls,
Which shine as the true homes of creativity.
Poetry cannot be found solely in music or rhythm;
Those are just vehicles for it.
Poetry is life painted in more bearable colors—
A truth that doesn't suffocate with self-righteousness.
It embodies both philosophy and something beyond it;
It is a science more precise than science itself.
Its nourishment comes directly from the ultimate source—
Poetry is the food, the air, the earth, both new and old;
Its message is understandable, even when it appears obscure.
Poetry is weary and seeks fresh perspectives,
Exploring new emotions
To create new pathways for communication.
It doesn't require excessive baggage

If its purpose remains clear,

Whether on paper or in the digital world.

Poetry no longer needs to rely on rhymes;

It doesn't have to be remembered

Through the repetition of refrains

But instead, through the recurrence of light.

POEMS

Some poems are a joy to read,

While others provoke deep reflection.

Some help us discover ourselves,

While others find us unexpectedly.

Some are hidden away,

While others remain open and clear.

The best poems don't explicitly teach us;

Even when they do, they invite us to look beyond language

To access a deeper source of knowledge

That many people already understand.

This understanding is felt rather than articulated—

Experienced in the gut rather than through words.

Some poems are like spells,

While others resemble stories.

Some are like volcanoes,

Seemingly feeding the fountains of paradise.

Some poems are pure sounds,

While others embody the essence of poetry itself.

Some poems are a joy to read,

And some inspire deep reflection.

Some we discover, and some find us.

Some are hidden away,

While others remain open and clear.

SUMMER BY THE SEA

The sea gently pulses,
Carrying the sweet scent of summer
To the city bathed in the glow
Of streetlamps. The music is loud.

Women move gracefully,
Their alluring fragrances blending
With the aroma of summer in the city.

Confusion builds and intensifies
As summer sweeps over the sea,
Filling this vibrant and cheerful place.

Untamed desires immerse themselves in the froth
Of summer's magic force,
Pulling them deeper into the night.

The music grows louder,
And you know how it goes
When the ghostly summer wind
Draws everyone into the bubbling pot of heated cravings.

SUMMER AND WINTER

Summer or winter depends on our mood,
On the music we listen to,
On the city we inhabit and the people around us,
On our connection to the sky,
On the memories we recall from our travels
Through various towns and landscapes,
Through the tranquility of an oasis,
Through the chaos of our thoughts,
Through wild nights and dreams.
Summer or winter, spring or fall—
These are not just the seasons
But the states of our minds.

(LOST) HISTORY

The interpretation of events often obscures history
With fragments of taste and peculiarities
Captured by historians, rulers, and sycophants alike.
The truth can be beguiling and distant despite our efforts.
What truly matters is not the accuracy
Of the truth or the falsehood itself,
But the motivations behind each narrative.
An unyielding life shapes these motivations,
Compelling individuals to accept an imposed truth
Rather than navigate the barren landscape
Of lost and silenced history.

MAGICAL BOX

Even when we travel far away,
We never truly leave behind the familiar places and faces.
They linger over the snowy mountaintops,
Bringing with them the scent of linden trees,
Accompanied by the lights of houses that resemble stars,
Scattered just enough along the roads at night.
We watched these lights through the window
As our parents drove us toward new experiences,
From which we remember only the glow.

A faithful friend follows us wherever we go—a magical box
Full of essential items and various treasures.
It holds fragrances, ornaments, scars, and a few grains of wisdom.
From this box, we occasionally pull out memories:
An almost forgotten spring,
A flower given to an unknown lady,
An old, adorned drinking fountain near the park
In the city we once called home;
The music that still plays from within the box,
And the eyes that once captivated us.

There are cafés, streetlamps, and little springs
Where we drank water along the way

To the sea—a destination we eagerly awaited every year.
All of this continues to live on in the magical box,
As the little Sun shines over the picturesque landscapes
Awakening almost forgotten sounds and memories.

If we seem to lose these memories,
They never lose us; they linger and eventually find us,
Whether we are in a desert
Or deep in the heart of a jungle.
We can still hear the music from the magical box—
Fountains in the desert garden.
Even when we travel far away,
The magical box remains,
Pulling us back without warning.

CLICHÉS

I was eager to share

The most important thing with her,

But it felt like a cliché.

The words shouted in my head,

Yet even that felt cliché as well.

I tried to come up with something better,

Only to find myself stuck in another cliché.

I shook my head, closed my eyes, and prayed—

Once again, it was cliché upon cliché.

Finally, a tear slipped from my eye,

And she understood,

Even though a tear is a cliché too.

YOU ARE HOPE

When I speak the truth,

You claim it is a judgment rather than the truth.

When I share white lies,

You say they are just fantasies.

When I try to express something

I can't fully articulate,

You say I am simply rambling.

When I speak to share,

You tell me I talk too much.

Yet, I keep trying to convey

What I need to share—

Something that I can't repeat endlessly,

So, I cover it with words and fantasies,

Because if I attempted to express the real meaning

Of what I truly want to say without words,

It would strip away all its significance.

THE GREATEST ARTISTS AND SCIENTISTS

The first pioneers spoke,
Trailblazers who sketched the first curves of the alphabet,
Bravely ventured into the unknown,
Building bridges of language and awakening dormant minds.

Yet often, the most significant pioneers—
The unseen visionaries and silent heroes—
Fade into the shadows, their names lost to time,
Frozen on the silent lips of history.

In the tumult of past events, they remain overlooked—
Unrecognized giants, part of the silent
Collective genius of humanity
Shining like invisible stars hidden by darkness.

Without their courage, where would we be today?
Each letter and every word serves as a testament to their legacy.

WAITING ROOM

WAITING ROOM

A terrifying scream or a gentle whisper,
Waiting in the dark.

A troubling thought,
Wrapped in the velvety fabric of language.

An omen of boredom,
Lurking in the mud.

Bliss in the vacuum
Of the waiting room,

Where a flower grows.

THE UNKNOWN

Apparitions, clouds, and fog;
Unknown faces in unfamiliar places
That somehow feel familiar.

Unknown shapes and elements,
Unknown feelings and thoughts
Have strangely become familiar.

Unknown sciences, teachings, and laws,
Obscure figures and undiscovered teachers
In some way feel familiar.

An unknown past, present, and future
Lived without understanding,
Yet still feel familiar.

Even you, unknown to yourself,
Wonder and gaze at a world
Designed to feel familiar.

THE SHADOW OF DEATH

What is it that follows you
Like a shadow not cast by light?

Inside your being,
It lingers.

An invisible shadow,
Stronger than life.

A shadow living within a shadow,
An animal without teeth,

Biting slowly into a shadowy realm,
With the patience of a predator.

Bloodthirsty patience
That promises eternal life.

SOME OBJECTS OF ART

Even the overlooked object
Fights for its place.

It has survived many bruises,
Living on through its scars.

It was the labor, disguised as love,
That gave it life.

Still, it cries out,
Drawing attention to its scars.

Lame and sterile,
Yet, it yearns for vitality.

Hungrily and jealously, it moves
Through the crowds of other objects.

It spreads a silent message:
"Look at me; beauty is boring."

CONTAMINATED MINDS

Born from despair,

They become magnets for disaster.

Eager for attention,

They create situations just to be noticed.

Thriving on misery,

They poison and dilute joy.

Although they claim to cure madness,

They only produce more chaos.

They multiply at an alarming rate,

Abundant yet easily spread.

Emerging from broken hearts,

They act like invisible, incurable viruses.

Their goal is to find a place in others' hearts

To form a large, contaminated family,

Born from their despair.

NEW MAN

Fly toward the inner sky to reach the outer sky.

Consider the Moon merely a first station.

Listen to the emptiness to find your way.

Travel through memory to discover the future.

Learn from the distance that touches the horizon,

From which the mountain grows, splitting the sky into two.

Be that mountain, embracing new planets and territories.

Domesticate places whose names you do not know.

Name the future after yourself.

Give birth to the grassy fields

Of the new landscapes you create and cultivate.

Define reality and the gap between yourself and the world.

Rename the sky and the Universe.

Offer enchantments and songs to every piece of ground you enrich.

Conceive a new language more powerful than one made of words.

Think, sing, and communicate without words or music.

Make the world sing and talk to you.

Become a listener of spheres,

A listener of waves traveling through space,

A listener of unheard music.

Become an angel whose wings guard the edges of your garden.

Bring with you all your knowledge, history, and heritage.

Build a new family stemming from the old one.

Bring discoveries, artefacts, songs, and books—

Bring it all and share it widely.

Offer gifts ranging from roses to diamonds

Or whatever you have,

For the Ultimate Lady—Existence.

Charm her with all your spells;

To win her heart, you must earn her trust.

Do not be too shy around her.

Share everything you know, even your secret plans and mischief.

She will listen to you,

Even when you speak something outrageous.

Once you find a place in her heart,

Your entire journey will be etched there,

And you will uncover the true meaning of your experience.

GREATNESS

You become a slave to anything you hoard.
Unchain yourself from the burdens of ownership;
By doing so, you become the true master of yourself,
Which is the most valuable possession in the Universe.

Vanity acts as an emotional scarecrow, driving people away.
Do not feel diminished by your insignificance.
Avoid striving for greatness solely for the sake of being great,
Unless it serves the purpose of helping others.

Help others recognize their value.
By assisting them, you become a part of their lives.
You become more of yourself
When you allow others to be themselves.

There is no greatness greater than the wisdom
Gained from modesty in the presence
Of the magnificent Universe of which you are a part.
Yet, you remain yourself, enriched by the whole world.

BONFIRE LOG

I willingly give you my heart,
Which you turned into a bonfire log
To warm your cold soul.

THE WAY

Nothing grows outward;
It only grows inward.
The way out is within.

You are both the traveler and the Path.
There is no you outside of yourself.
(You are your own Path.)

CRYSTALS OF FIRE

POOR UTTERANCES

Aim to speak more thoughtfully,
But don't hold back
When your voice truly needs to be heard.

If you choose to wait
For a moment of significance or a pivotal event,
Remember that it may not arrive as you hope.

What could be more valuable than the beauty
That comes from your desire to articulate your feelings,
Before they fade into silence?

You can convey your emotions and needs
Without resorting to outbursts, tears, pleas,
Or using less effective words.

LION AND ZEBRA

The zebra runs alongside other zebras,
Galloping with a trembling heart.
Her black-and-white stripes
This time attract death.
Bewilderment fills her as dust swirls around,
But it's all in vain; she cannot escape.
The lion's gaze cannot be deceived,
For what it sees is neither black nor white,
But red.

DNA AND BEAUTY

Would there be beauty without color?
Would all the shapes blend
Into an unrecognizable mass?

What is beauty?
Is it defined by the richness of color,
Or perhaps by shape, sound, or smell?

The dilemma remains: is beauty deserved,
Or is it merely a random consequence
Of accidental causes and events?

There would be no beauty
Without a universal algorithm that creates it,
Shaping and reshaping all
That flows through the DNA.

MESSAGES

Waves are messages

Sent into space.

They are not just forms of energy;

Instead, they encompass the entirety of knowledge

From both the past and the future.

Yet, they overflow with freedom,

Unbound by determinism.

An entire infinity exists

Within a small message, confined

In immeasurable space

Beyond our comprehension.

This reality is shaped by the freedom

That thrives within the determinism

Of an undetermined infinity,

Rich with inexhaustible possibilities.

UNIVERSAL BATTLE

Without conflict, nothing holds true meaning.
Even in love, differing elements clash.
Everything is at odds with everything else,
Creating a constant struggle—even during times of peace.
These periods serve as moments for rest and recovery.

Most often, the battles we face are not intentional;
Rather, they arise from a struggle between energies
Striving to survive and find harmony.
We aim to crystallize our understanding
Through constant examination,
Sifting through excess and eliminating
What does not contribute to our idea of progress.

This pursuit leads to breakthroughs
That grant us freedom from the constraints of instincts,
Outdated beliefs, and the burdens
Imposed by biology, history, and geography.

CRYSTALS OF FIRE

Flowery Sun,
Without fragrance,
Gives birth to flowers of emptiness.

From its hot heart,
Sunny petals grow,
Explosively majestic.

His Majesty—the Sun,
Her Majesty—the Flower,
Two in one—one in two.

Lustrous petals—crystals of fire,
Dancing with the planets,
Warming the cold and lonely night.

WHERE DID THEY GO

All the people who still live in our memories—
Where have they gone?
Memories rush into oblivion,
Filled with battles and friendships.
All the loves, tragedies, and histories—
Dead stars and alien civilizations fade away—
Just like the summers spent by the sea
That once felt so real and enduring.

CHOOSE WHAT SILENCE CHOOSES

Love me not for what I have done;
That is merely an act of courage.

Love me not for what I have learned;
That is simply knowledge.

Love me not for what I have said;
That is just talent—
A skill or a moment of sincerity.

Love me not for any obvious reason;
That is just a reason.

Instead, love me for what I have never said—
For what silence chooses to reveal,
For what only silence truly understands.

MAN-MADE GOD

Horses gallop,
Red, white, black, and pale.
Thunderous mountains rise
With divine words in visions—
Stronger than words or swords,
Stronger than emperors or reason.
Enslaved by reality,
In which believers dwell,
A man created a nightmarish God
In his own image.

CONQUERORS

They will come again; they always do.
This time, they will be more articulate and polished.
They won't just take; they will also give.
They will be more dangerous.

Nobody will recognize them.
No one will know where they come from
Or what they truly want.
They will arrive as friends—
Generous and welcoming.

Instead of taking gold,
They will bring gold, silver, and money.
They possess it all.
There is still something they do not own: You.
This time, they will come for your soul.

A FLOWER IN EMPTINESS

FAKE AVANT-GARDE

If we all claimed to know everything,
Nobody would truly understand anything.

The right to beauty stems from genuine knowledge,
Embraced by an anarchist dilettante
Who proclaimed the right of ugliness
To exist as ugliness
And the right of ugliness
To also be beautiful.

Who decided and declared
The different types of beauty and knowledge—
Ugly beauty or beautiful ugliness—
A flower without a scent,
Burnt petals, muddy colors,
Iron spikes instead of thorns,
Blooming in their democratic right.

Ugliness seeks an easier path to beauty,
But beauty had to pay a hefty price to earn its place
In the hierarchy of valued ideals.

SAYING IT WITHOUT SAYING IT

Tricky words can obscure true meaning.
Genuine feelings often express themselves through what remains.
If a single word could encapsulate love,
It might not convey much value.

Wrapped within a small, unspoken sentiment,
True meaning can communicate without the need for words.
The essence of the world can be contained
Within a single, unexpressed feeling.

The core of life often resides
In the simplest, one-syllable expressions.
Even if feelings are left unspoken,
Their true significance can still resonate.

Instead of relying on words,
Let your actions illuminate and enlighten the world.

LOVE EQUATION

I am fading away inside you,
While you thrive within me.
As I perish, my love deepens;
The flower of death embraces life.
In dying, I discover life—
A vibrant force that nourishes passionate love.
You are a river, a sky in my thoughts.
I swim through the currents in my veins,
Striving to reach the sky.
In dying, I am blossoming;
In living, you warm my life,
Nurtured by your love.

BOILING POT

It requires more energy to hate than to love.
Hate has to invent reasons,
Similar to water in the desert
Of a thirsty mind.
It is a boiling pot
Ready to explode
At anyone who hates to hate.

FLOWER IN EMPTINESS

It's not just the words that go unsaid;

It's the events, the experiences, the mysteries.

It's not the music that remains unwritten;

It's the whispers of the Universe.

It's not the feelings that cry;

It's the love that faded from love.

It's not death that waits;

It's life in disguise.

It's not memory that is lost;

It's the rebirth of the known in the unknown.

It's not the vicious cycle of life;

It's the circle of possibilities.

It's not the repetition of what is possible;

It's the rendition of the impossible.

It's not merely what is possible;

It's the infinite nature of the impossible.

It is the cosmic Flower in emptiness,

Growing from nowhere into nowhere.

CASTLES

How difficult it is to touch the horizon,
To see the other side of reality.
We dream of dreams, endlessly dreaming,

Inside the castle where the secret library is hidden,
Within the womb of a dream, in the embrace of a ghost.
This castle grows within us, revealing

What we cannot see, yet still
Offering glimpses of all the dreams
Stored in the books of a library we seek.

We dream on the road toward the castle,
In a labyrinth filled with birds, animals,
Insects, plants, planets, stars, galaxies, and universes.

We yearn for new light, new vision,
A new touch in a more harmonious world,
As we gaze upon the brightest light of flight.

Walking through this very dream,
Unique among all in the vast labyrinth,
We are the castles we are searching for.

PARKS AND STREETS

While he walks down the street, he thinks of other streets—
Perhaps one in Florence, Paris, or New York.
He reflects on the beauty yet to be discovered
And continues to walk, dream, and ponder.

Parks embody a universal quality;
They are tranquil oases
Set apart from the noisy surroundings—
A true heaven in the urban jungle.
Though cities differ greatly,
All parks share a similar essence.

In one park, he encountered a love
He had lost in another park.
To get from one park to the next,
He had to traverse various streets.
These streets spanned different time zones,
Yet all the parks occupied the same temporal space.

He began to feel diminished
And started moving faster through the streets,
Which began to blend into a single avenue.

It was neither the Champs-Élysées nor Boulevard Saint-Michel,

Nor was it Park Avenue or Fifth Avenue.

It was not Michigan Avenue in Chicago,

Avenida 9 de Julio in Buenos Aires,

Piazza del Popolo or Piazza Venezia in Rome,

Palazzo della Signoria in Florence,

Campo dei Santi Giovanni e Paolo in Venice,

Corso Vittorio Emanuele II in Milan,

Parliament Street in Exeter, England,

Prince Michael Street in Belgrade,

Or Red Square in Moscow.

It was a blend of all these avenues,

Leading him to the park he discovered

While he wasn't actively searching for it.

He found it as he walked down a street he thought he did not like,

Evoking strange thoughts in unfamiliar lands.

CHURCH ON THE HILL

There is a Church on the hill
In which no one ever prays.

Or perhaps you are the Church
To which you direct your prayers,

Trying to climb unknown hills,
Deciphering dreamlike visions.

God is searching for you,
But you are a runaway.

THE SECRET OF THE WHOLE ONE

I am real, even though I am not.
Such a sweet contradiction:
To be the one who exists
And yet the one who does not.

I soared to the depths of emptiness
And kissed the light
With the lips of darkness, and I returned
While remaining in the same place.

When you are, you are not,
And when you are not, you are.
That is the secret of the Whole One,
Which is and is not.

OUTCAST

The Earth is a round dream, and the Sun is another.
Both exist side by side in the vast expanse of the Universe.
Roundness dances upon itself while flatness stretches out,
Creating distance—a newly formed space and a fresh dimension.
The horizon extends far, lost in its infinity.

The Sun remains, and the Earth stands fixed.
There is no revolution, no rotation,
Yet, the Sun circles the Earth, and the Earth orbits the Sun,
Together, they journey through the Milky Way,
While our galaxy spins around a central black hole,
Its majestic, invisible light glows deep within.

Where do flatness and roundness meet?
What lies at the heart of circularity within this hollow sphere?

In this circle of emptiness, a phantom atom struggles,
Seeking its place in the vast nothingness.
Space is not merely space; it is a void,
Seduced by its own curves, encircling a hollow sphere,
Wrapped in layers of emptiness.
This creates a relentless cycle of circularity, being, and non-being.

THE HOME OF THE WORLD

SONGS OF LIGHT

SONG OF LIGHT

The grass is less green now,
Air is less fresh, and even the blue is less blue.

I don't go to the shore anymore
To watch the sea embrace the light,

To ask the Sun a new question.
I'm losing an old friend;

He used to tell me stories
In gentle whispers through the light.

"Sun, shine upon him," I heard a voice in the air,
"He is blind without you and feels lost;

Give him back his sight,
Grant him fresh air and restored senses;

Let him see, hear, smell, feel, and breathe;
Give him back his wings and let him fly toward you again."

SONG IN THE GARDEN

Come to my secret Oasis, she said,

To see my flowers,

To listen to my birds.

Come to my Oasis

To admire my fountains,

To see the sounds and hear the light,

To experience my uniquely mixed world,

To inhale the colors and fragrances,

And tell me what you feel

When you see the light in my eyes,

When you listen to the silent sounds.

Come to my Oasis, she said.

SONG OF ELYSIUM

On the bridges, in the parks and gardens,
In the places where we don't expect it, bliss happens,

Sinking into silence,
We attune ourselves to the secret language,

By recognizing each other
In every song and face, every scent and sound.

We listen to the trembling beat in our chests.
It never lies.

We listen as our senses awaken and sharpen.
They never lie.

We see the Elysium,
And we slowly walk in.

A SONG WITHIN A SONG

We traveled a long way and forgot
The reason for the invention of poetry.
It is a prayer, a sacrifice,
And a means of purification.

Poetry served to attract rain,
To invoke the presence of God,
Or to seek guidance
On unpromising, gloomy mornings.

It is a miracle, a magical sound,
It is a remedy and a soothing balm.

THE DREAM SONG

Sing with your full voice
And let your melody grow within me;

Then fly down until you reach the bottom,
Searching to find me;

Wake me with your song,
Then, soar back to the heights,

Sing from your distant heights,
Wave to me and show me the way;

Look for me everywhere,
And share what you uncover while searching;

Sing with your full voice,
And travel through the world to find me;

I have been waiting for you in storms,
Waiting for you in sadness,

And in dreams, for
You were my destination;

Dream for me and sing,

For I have been asleep for so long;

Come to my dreams to find me,

So we can dream awake and together.

Awaken me from awakeness

So I can dream an absolute dream.

AWAKENING

GOD

I see your science—
A simple discovery—
You are me, and I am you.

Words, words, words;
Too many words
Obstruct the way

To simple discoveries.

ETERNAL FATHER

Come closer, distant creature;
Let me see your face.
Come closer, even if your light
Or darkness may destroy me.

It is not a fair game,
Following wrong steps
Into the dead ends
Of an endless labyrinth.

Come closer, wild Spirit,
Even as a chimera or mirage;
Let me see your face,
My dearest friend and father.

AWAKENING

Why deceive
Flying into new territories
Without being ready?

Why dream
Without understanding
New revelations?

Why know
Without feeling
The simple joy of awakening?

Why wake
Without burning?

CURE

With every revelation,

We believed we had discovered the truth

Beyond mere words,

Finding solace only

In phrases that had the power

To heal our souls.

PRETENSE

Why all the noise,
All that pretense?
Talks of glory—if

Beyond words and fame,
There lives a simple world,
Equally generous to all.

SOUL OF THE UNKNOWN

Who are you?
Eternity asks.

I am the wave of the soul
And the soul of the wave.

Of what? Eternity asks.
Of the unknown, Darkness replied.

THE EAGLE AND THE FATA MORGANA

I WAS AN EAGLE

In my dream, I was an eagle soaring,
Accompanied by soft clouds.
I watched them flee, disappearing,
Finding a new home for life.
In my dream, I was a dream.

A whisper echoed through the void,
Moving swiftly through space.
I was that whisper, dreaming the dreamer's dream.
His magic force kept me dreaming;
In his dream, I am a dream.

SECRET KNOWLEDGE

I never know where my knowledge comes from,
Or what purpose it serves.
If only I could understand the true reason,
I could endure more easily
As I seek to discover and reveal
The secret, whose distant flame I sense.

OTHER PLACES

Tell me about other places,
The driving force of the Universe,
Holding more to explore than dreams
That blind us, turning thoughts into verse.

Tell me of other senses,
Other dimensions that remain unseen:
Beyond death, there is more awaiting us,
More than we could ever agree on.

AN ORDINARY DAY

Everything felt ordinary:

People walked along crowded streets,

Women flaunted their tanned legs,

Casual glances drew attention

From both lazy men and those in a hurry.

Children played in the yards,

Yelling and scoring in their games.

It was just an ordinary day filled with small rewards.

On the beach, basking in the sunshine,

The noise grew louder

From people playing volleyball,

Earning applause here and there,

In a day that revealed little

About how important it all truly was.

PARKS AND STREETS

As he walks down the street, he thinks of another—
Perhaps one in Florence, Paris, or New York.
He reflects on the beauty yet to be discovered
And continues to walk, dream, and think.

Parks embody a universal quality;
They are tranquil oases
Separated from their noisy surroundings,
Like heaven in a human jungle.
Although cities differ greatly,
All parks share a similar essence.

In one park, he experienced the love
He had lost in another.
To get from one park to another,
He had to traverse various streets.
These streets lay in different time zones,
Yet all the parks existed in the same temporal space.

He began to feel diminished
And started moving faster through the streets,
Which began to blend into a single avenue.
It was not the Champs-Élysées or Boulevard Saint-Michel,

Nor was it Park Avenue or Fifth Avenue.

It was not Michigan Avenue in Chicago,

Avenida 9 de Julio in Buenos Aires,

Piazza del Popolo or Piazza Venezia in Rome,

Palazzo della Signoria in Florence,

Campo dei Santi Giovanni e Paolo in Venice,

Corso Vittorio Emanuele II in Milan,

Parliament Street in Exeter, England,

Prince Michael Street in Belgrade,

Or Red Square in Moscow.

It was all the avenues combined

Leading toward the park, he discovered

While he wasn't actively looking for it

As he walked down a street, he thought he did not like.

Strange thoughts revived in unfamiliar lands.

ROSEBUD IN A FAIRY TALE

ROSEBUD

Don't say a word;
A rose blooms in silence.

Protect it from the wind,
From the crowd and the noise.

Only let the light in
And allow the ground to do its work.

Wait patiently
Until you see the Rosebud.

UNCERTAINTY

He was heading in the wrong direction,
Unaware of it.

It was too late to turn back,
And staying put seemed like the better option.

Not long after, he noticed
Many people were going the same way.

Curious, he asked why they were taking this route.
They replied, "To escape."

"From what?" he wondered.
"From boredom and uncertainty," they said.

TEMPLE OF HOPE

We declare: We are the ones
Who will build the Temple of Hope,
To remember that the sky is blue,
To listen to the whispers of the ocean,
And to find joy in the wonders of life.

You say:
You will not change anything;
The world will remain the same.
It is what it is.

Yet, there is still hope
That this will not just be a war of words.

DEEDS

Her deeds had wings;
They soared and took on a life of their own.
Rewarded with laughter and wisdom,
Encouraged and healed,
She developed her own wings,
Flying toward the land
Of hidden wisdom and knowledge.
And she never spoke of it.

VICTORY

Victories need no explanations.
Winners understand there is no true winning;
They do what must be done.

True victories are felt rather than announced.
Trophies cannot measure genuine victories.
Wisdom is the ultimate triumph

If true wisdom is even possible
To achieve or recognize.

NOWHERE

In striving for perfection,

He mastered the art of anonymity,

Became imperceptible

And arrived from nowhere to nowhere.

EARLY RETIREMENT

He was a well-behaved child.
Many saw him as a born philosopher.
He had answers to nearly everything
And retired at an early age.

VANITY

How many stories would remain unwritten
Or inventions never created?

How many battles would not have been won?
How many temples would not have been built?

How many women would be less happy,
And how many would be much happier?

How many songs would go unheard,
While quarrels could have been avoided?

How much more stable would we be,
And how much closer to one another,

Without vanity?

TOO LATE

They spoke of eternity,
But their actions were temporary.

They spoke of wisdom,
Yet their actions were damaging.

They spoke of brotherhood,
And the outcome was division.

And now,
It's too late.

YOU KNOW IT, YOU FEEL IT

What are you searching for—
Do you know?
What are you longing for—
Do you feel?

What makes you feel this—
Do you know?
What makes you know this—
Do you feel?

You know it by feeling;
You feel it by knowing.

MEANING

I cannot teach you anything, the teacher said.

Just open your eyes.

MY OTHER SELF

I am a slave to desire,
I am a slave to pride,
I am a slave to vice,
I am a slave to success.

"Get rid of desire," Desire said.
"Get rid of pride," Pride said.
"Get rid of vices," Honor said.
"Get rid of competition," Success said.

I will still be a slave to sin,
A slave to materialism,
A slave to love,
A slave to myself.

"Get rid of sin and lust,
Of materialism and love,
And you will get rid of yourself,"
Said my other self.

"Are you proposing suicide?" I asked sadly.
"No, I would never suggest that," my other self replied.
"Then what are you trying to say?"
"Just be yourself," said my other self.

POETS

WALT WHITMAN

Captain, our captain,
We take your hand,
Following in your footsteps on the streets
Of Chicago, New York, and San Francisco.

Your spirit rises from the grassy fields,
Appearing on the horizon
As a beam of light signaling to America,
Reminding her of her roots.

We follow a trail of light.
Leading to forgotten springs,
Placing our ears on the ground
To get closer to the leaves of grass and listen

With a desire to understand transformed America.

A LETTER TO EMILY DICKINSON

A word thrown into silence
Always finds its echo somewhere,
Where silence opens hidden lexicons,
And words return to silence,
Arriving at just the right moment.

WILLIAM BUTLER YEATS

To achieve the simplicity
Of words that have learned to dance
Without much support from a dancer
Who mastered the steps of a worthy life
From those who excelled in the art of dance.
Is it a dance or the act of dancing?
Is it to live or to be lived?
It is not the dancer but the dance;
It is not life but the living mind,
The truth of existence found in dance.
If he had chosen only to live,
The dance would have been much less lively.

A great dancer follows the steps
Only life knows how to choreograph.

ROBERT FROST

At the crossroads, there is a word
That signifies the open road ahead.
A song is rising from the dark woods
Of expanding, equally perilous cities.

A vast family rides on horses,
Traveling along different paths,
Exploring and discovering why
One road is better than another.

A word sent to open the road
Transforms that road into a melodic path;
The road chooses the rider,
And the song becomes the journey.

A word that opens the road
Allows the road to sing the rider's song.

WALLACE STEVENS

The sea was a house, and the world was a ship.
You were both the sea and the ship.

The ship was stormy, while the sea was calm,
And the house waited for the world

To arrive by way of the ship on the sea.
The sea was a ship, and the world was a house.

You were the ship in the sea—
The house and the world.

The world was the ship in the sea,
And the sea was inside the house.

THE UNUSUAL LOVE SONG OF T. S. ELIOT

At twenty-six, I was inexperienced;
Still, I knew a lot about love
In the wasteland of reasoning.
It's not important when you start
Practicing, but rather when you begin searching.
I committed myself to finding love
Before others even knew it existed, *breeding*

Lilacs out of the dead land, mixing
My thoughts, my longings, my love
For something that didn't need naming.
In the misty mornings, I recognized
The dew on the petals, alive yet sleepy.
I was a dreamer, I admit, thinking,
April is the cruelest month, flying

Thoughts about some distant teaching,
Seeing the invisible in the visible, loving
Wild ideas that make love, searching
To find it; love was a secret hard to decode—
Sacred to me, it was. Students talked
Of business, Dante, and Michelangelo;
That was important, yet not so vital

In the land where death died long ago, blooming

Roses taught me a lesson, awakening

The land where human measures are important

Yet not so crucial, so I stayed, deserving

A degree from real roses, forgetting

The Ph.D. that was waiting for me at Harvard.

Yet, it was not about Michelangelo,

But does it matter? I saw paintings

And landscapes—both dead lands and alive ones—

Understanding that feeling is more important than knowing.

I had everything in my head,

And I remained in a place where dreaming

Was more important than competing

In the land where women come and go, talking

Of Sarah Bernhardt and Coco Chanel in the Sistine Chapel,

And men come and go, talking

About wars. Children come and go, talking

Of chocolate, and they all go, leaving

Not much to ponder when exchanging

Experiences with feelings, transforming

Experiences into meanings, mixing

Thoughts about love evaporating

Into "the yellow fog that rubs its back upon the window panes,
The yellow smoke that rubs its muzzle on the window panes;"
And in the end, I understood April, learning
That April seemed cruel only in the dead land, knowing
That every month is equally paradisiacal and hellish,
Equally paradoxical.

e. e. cummings

there may be greater poets, perhaps
but there is only one cummings.

to be nobody but yourself
is indeed the hardest fight.

Plato did not say this
or we wouldn't believe it.

he heard us in the silence
unknowingly, we spoke to him, and

he sent us an old word
flying over the new yet unnamed avenue.

we heard him whispering
Avenue of Love,

and we promised, under his spell of love,
to never tell.

THE WAY

THE WAY

The tree—
Growing from nowhere
Into nowhere

Between nowhere
And nowhere—
The Way

THE WAY AND THE TRUTH

In the beginning,
There was an overwhelming loneliness.

Truth took the first step
And began to listen to its own footsteps.

That's how the conversation started,
Making loneliness more bearable.

As Truth moved further
The path became brighter.

Then, Truth began to listen
To how the Way communicates.

The Way became the only path,
The sole purpose of Truth.

As a result, the Truth and the Way
Became one and the same.

BEING AND NOTHING

Time and space are void;
This should be obvious.

Nothing is simply nothing,
Which means it is void.

If Being lacks space,
Then it, too, must be nothing.

Time, space, and nothing
Are all the same.

If time, space, and nothing are indeed nothing,
Then, nothing can be new.

There is no concept of old and new
In nothing.

Everything must be both
Old and new at the same time.

If there is no space and no time,
Where are we, and where are we going?

Is Being hidden within space?
Or does space exist within Being?

Who is fighting against whom?
Who is stronger?

Does Being enter space,
Or does space enter Being?

THE WAY BACK

From the Darkness I came,
Traveling a long way.

I am here now
To stay for a while,
But then I must find the way back.

SHELL

I am the largest and the smallest—
The shell of the Universe.

BLACK STARS

BEFORE AND AFTER

Before the first before
And after the last after
There is night waiting,

Almost nonexistent
Yet so constant
Night in the Heart of Light.

IN THE HEART OF THE NIGHT

Before it was born
The day was darker than the night.
It held the whole Darkness

Within itself,
And from its dark Heart
The Light shone.

THE NIGHT IS ALWAYS AWAKE

When the whole world is sleeping,
The night remains awake, faithfully waiting.

There is nothing more faithful than the night.
Nothing can escape its eternal love.

ETERNITY

Black stars in black waters.
Black emptiness
Swallowed by black Light.

White Light emerges
From the black stars
In the black sea.

White swallows black;
Then, black swallows white
For all eternity.

FAIRY TALE

Shining dots in the sky—
White holes in the black sea—
Doors to an old home,

A distant place—
Enlightened joy
Eternal bliss.

With lost reality,
Distant, yet present, desire
Craves to merge.

HOME

There is only one home,
Only one story to tell,
Only One Way
To one destination.

There is only one Harbor,
Only one shining Heart,
Where all the suns are born.

That is our Home.

THE HOME OF THE WORLD

ONE WORLD—ONE HOME—ONE MIND

Stormy oceans give birth to the Light.
Nights are remnants of that Light,
Leftovers of darkness as the world is born
From a hellish kiss of Darkness and Light.

Life is a destination,
The reason to fall and rise,
The reason to reinvent the same,
The world within the world.

Death is as necessary as life,
Darkness is needed to see the Light,
Tears are not the enemies of smiles;
The only path is connection.

We live in death and die in life,
May see in darkness and be blinded by light.
We laugh and cry together,
Through this day and this night.

THE SPIRIT OF THE WORLD

I

The world is my embrace of the unknown,
A fusion of my spirit, soul, and essence—
My enduring hope.

The world is my cherished companion,
Filled with love and challenges—
The journey of my life.

The world is my Infinite Ocean and tranquil Island,
The guiding lighthouse—
My blooming rose.

The world flows through my veins,
With stars as its blood cells—
It is my only chance.

The world reflects my vision, holds my memories,
Captures your essence—
It grants me wings to soar.

The world is my flourishing garden,
Rich with diverse flora and fauna—
It is my Kingdom of Growth.

The world is my source of harmony, a book waiting to be
   unlocked,
A whisper eager to be heard—
It is my paradise.

The world embodies my fire, stirring passions and desires,
Fuelling my will to thrive—
It tests my resilience.

The world represents my struggle for rebirth,
Bridging endings and new beginnings—
It is my purgatory of transformation.

The world nourishes my breath,
Offering salvation even in solitude—
It is my precious time.

The world is my light bulb, casting brilliance into space,
Embodying love and illuminating the path to life—
It is my Masterpiece.

The world invites me to walk into the night,
To seek the light and share my journey—
It is my Way.

The world blossoms with an array of colors,
A garden of red, white, yellow, and black roses shimmering in
    darkness—
It is my home of stars.

The world is my home and a lighthouse of hope for all.

II

Spirit of the Universe awakens with the thunder,
Measured by the sound of light,
It embodies its children in the world;
They are its life.

Omnipresent emptiness,
Lonely space in waiting;
Its atoms and galaxies
Are whispers in the night.

As it travels through itself,
Its waves crash against the dual shores
Of loneliness, falling
Into empty necessity.

It gives birth to space
By inhaling and exhaling.
Its only desire
Is to live and never die.

Its love is life;
Its life is love:
Two truths from the same dream;
Darkness is merely the other side.

It sets in motion
A multitude from oneness,
A majestic competition
Of life in movement.

It allows them to fight
To create order;
It permits them to consume each other
To maintain it.

It is the thunder;
They are its light.
There is no evil,
Except for the cost of motion.

It makes the oceans
And creates the shores.
It is the darkness
Born of light.

It is old—
Older than darkness,
Older than light,
Darker than night.

It is the light,
Older than light.
We pay the price
For Its delight.

It disrupts the peace of nothingness,
The harmony of emptiness;
It thunders and bursts into the night.
All creation is almost diabolical.

Galaxies are the treetops of the invisible Universe.
There is no birth of anything
Without a pain,
There is no beauty without a price.

It is the Father, the Mother, and the Son.
There is no evil;
The devil is merely
The other face of God.

III

There is no outside,
No time or space beyond the Spirit of the Universe.
It is both the beginning and the end,
Yet, there is truly no beginning or end.

Only Its whispers,
Only the essence of Its desires.
There are no enemies, no colonies,
No emperors, no slaves.

Its thunder and Light
Are Its sight and hearing.
Its children are Its life.
It allows some to die so that others may live.

There is no hate
In the wars among Its children,
Only Its will and love
And their desire to survive.

There is no annihilation,
Only the formation
Of Its archipelago in an empty sea,
Its Island of multitude.

He nourishes Itself
By drawing space into Its core,
Growing not outward
But inward.

From Its thunders
Even Nothing is stirred;
From Its Light, Darkness hides;
From Its love, life is born.

Its love reflects It
Because It is love,
And Its love is formidable.
That is the price of life.

It soars and grows,
Moves back and forth.
It seeks to remember
And find Its way back.

There is no rebellion in Its dominion;
It is the only rebel.
There is no Lucifer
Or fallen angel.

It is the Bearer of Light;
It is the sole rebel.
It stole fire
From the selfish night.

It rebels against Darkness,
It disrupts her peace.
It is the fallen angel,
The very source of life.

It is Its creation.
It is the Creator of fire,
Of thunder, mist, and dust,
Of energy and elements.

It creates dragons and black holes.
It creates dark matter,
It creates circles and centrifuges.
Its truth can be Its deceit.

It creates blue skies,
Fresh air, and beauty.
Its beauty is as vast
As Its secrets, swimming in the night.

Its thunders are its revivals;

Its bursts are Its blood.
It flows through your veins;
It nourishes Itself on your journey.

It is both truth and lie;
It is the face never shown.
It rebels against the night.
Its Son shines upon It.

People call Its Son the devil,
But Spirit is reborn in multitude.
It is the Light you crave;
It is a life borne of love.

There is no devil, only the Spirit.
There is no duality, only unity.
The devil was born from weakness,
Not from the dream.

There is no thunder beyond love;
There is no hate in Light.
There is no motion without a price,
And the devil is Its own sacrifice.

There is only the Spirit
That shines upon the world and Itself.

There is only the Spirit whispering your Light
And our eyes and ears.

There is only the Spirit,
That sings in the night,
Only the Spirit
That loves to live and lives to love.

There is only the Spirit,
That never dies and always dreams
Of faith and salvation,
Of reasons to wake up and persist.

Its thunder is Its whisper;
Its life is the Light.
It is the only Father,
The Mother, and the Son.

Your translucent touch,
Its outstretched fingers,
Its omnipresent eye,
Its formidable force—tender and alive.

It is Its dream,
And Its dream dreams Itself.
It is the dream born from a dream,

And It lives Its dream.

It is the Creator;
It makes the world,
It dreams the world,
The world is Its dream.

It lives in dying;
It dies in living.
It is life and death;
It dies only to be reborn.

There is no death,
Only a moment of rest.
There is no end, only a new beginning.
The world never truly dies.

IV

When the Spirit embraces the darkness,
The darkness shines upon It.
When nights are not truly nights,
Loneliness is not loneliness.

When tomorrow is the same as yesterday,
Yesterday becomes tomorrow.
When tomorrow is merely a past dream,
Yesterday will be reborn.

When darkness longs for light,
Time comes into existence.
When time is compressed,
The world stands still.

When nights are lonely,
Loneliness feels dark.
When night is both day and night,
Emptiness seeks Spirit's light.

When Spirit creates an illusion,
It opens the Space.
When Space is open,
The Spirit is closer to itself the farther it goes.

When light cries for space,
Time is different here and there.
When space is both open and closed,
Spirit is both far and near.

When Spirit fills the circle,
It escapes from it.
When It circles the circle,
It becomes a circle.

When Spirit empties the circle,
It becomes a divider.
When It circles nothingness,
It deceives the night.

When Spirit takes flight,
It becomes a Composer.
When It circles the center,
Night consumes It.

When the world is born from loneliness,
Night transforms into light.
When the day is long and bright,
Light craves emptiness.

When Spirit unites with the night,
New stars are born.
When Spirit shines upon darkness,
It conquers the night.

When today emerges,
The night surrenders to the Spirit.
When It becomes the Master of the Night,
It is also its Light.

When there is no loneliness,
Everything is light.
When It becomes the light,
The light needs only itself.

When light unites with light,
Stars are born and die.
When It shines upon the light,
Spirit overpowers Itself.

When there is no birth,
Spirit yields to Itself.
When It is a slave to Itself,
It becomes the night of light.

When space cries for light,

Time remains the same everywhere.
When there is only open space,
Spirit is everywhere.

When It does not circle,
It is a wave.
When the center moves,
Everything becomes a code.

When everything is reminiscence,
Spirit is Its memory.
When waves become images,
Remembrance is the light.

When nothing moves,
All is an illusion.
When all is fire,
Fire becomes a dream.

When the dream is light,
Night must also dream.
When night seeks to ignite the fire,
Night becomes the Mother of Light.

When Light is the Father,
There are only two of them.

When the Father impregnates the Mother,
Spirit is both the Father and the Son.

When It is both the Father and the Mother,
The Son embodies both the Mother and the Father.
When nothing is everything,
Everything becomes a dream out of nothing.

(When there is no loneliness, loneliness is lonely.)

V

The Spirit rules and shines upon the night,
Dividing and uniting—
Devil and God in One,
It both gives and takes.

Born from Its desire,
It conquers Itself and gives birth to space.
It travels through Itself,
It is Its own space-time.

It is the Master conquered by Its Son.
It is Its reason, and It is Its life.
It is Its life, and It is Its dream.
It is the Alpha, and it is the Omega.

CHILDREN OF HOPE

They dwell within the Spirit,
And the Spirit dwells within them;
They are the thoughts of the Spirit,
And Spirit is their destination.

They are Spirit's blood,
Its floods and hurricanes,
Its nirvana and Its hell—
The voice of a multitude.

The voice of the voiceless,
Of the lost and forgotten,
Of the deaf and silent.
They are Its warriors and saints.

They are both mighty and meek;
They are emperors and beggars.
They possess everything and own nothing;
They are the architects of Its dreams.

They are the Masters, and Spirit is the servant;
It is the slaves who shape the Master.
They serve the Spirit by living Its life;

They are the guardians of Its aspirations.

They are Its hands and eyes,
Its Light and delight,
Its fire and growth—
Explosions that conquer the night.

They are alive and dead,
Awakened and asleep;
They create love and inspire destruction,
They exist within Its mind.

They are Its life and dream,
A prayer and a reason to be,
A joyful voice in the sorrowful night.

ALL WOMEN IN ONE

I SMELL YOU EVERYWHERE

The world blooms,
Words bloom;
Scents fill the air.

I see you blossoming,
Hear your winged words,
And smell you everywhere.

GARDEN OF LIGHT

A WOMAN IN THE GARDEN OF LIGHT

Longing to explore a hidden, sacred place,
I break through obstacles
To recognize the invisible sparks
Emanating from the precious discovery
Of the space between us,
Shining solely with longing.
I witness the awakening stars,
The birth of new landscapes,
Future cities, and temples,
I hear new stories falling
From the fountains of hidden art,
Where all the old sounds and colors
Transform into stars in the Garden.
And you—blindingly bright—
Melt me into new sensations
As I grow into the core,
With invisible roots that pierce,
Touching the essence of fire.
I traveled far to that place before space and time,
And return to this Garden to find you,
To see the real you, swimming
And flying ahead of the light
To discover you where the light never was
To learn that you are its source.

ALL WOMEN IN ONE

You shall not stop or hesitate
Until you pass through the forest,
And compare the beauty of day and night in summer—
Until you arrive in your own Ithaca.

There is always Venus,
A new Elissa to build a new Carthage,
A new Kingdom of Light.

You shall not stop until you find Venus:
One woman in all,
And all women in one.

Until you can say—*La Dolce Vita*,
Until you discover *Paradise Lost* in just one name,
Until you can say—
You are all women in one.

POETRY AND WOMEN

We no longer need to pray for rain,
Or petition the sky for more wheat, sugar, flour, and flowers.
We don't need to go to the Oracle of Delphi
Or seek to name new gods.

Yet, we still feel what our ancestors felt,
We still gaze at the same sky,
Smile at the same stars,
And listen to the same sea.

The essence of a woman has never changed.
Her role has shifted through different eras,
But a woman remains what she has always been—
Man's glory, destination, and dream.

As long as a woman breathes,
We will sing and send prayers to the gods and goddesses.
As long as she shines in our dreams,
We will listen to the winds carrying news on their lips.

We have attracted even more rain than we needed,
Creating and dismantling our gods.
We have sent our prayers to both old and new deities,

Born pagans, then baptized.

We have witnessed change—
Countries disappearing and new ones being born.
We have seen all metamorphoses, but not in her.
The song will never die.

You are a vestal virgin and a courtesan,
A famous star and a wild animal,
A reminder of bliss and a puzzle;
Nobody can tame you, only attain through fight.

You are Delilah and Judith,
A proud and dangerous black widow.
You are the industrious Elissa,
Waving from the shores of Carthage.

It must be that another
Has caught the vigor of Dido,
Heard her voice, and saw her silhouette in the blue
Beam over the sea, in the Mediterranean light.

(Godot is always waiting.
He is probably waiting for a woman.)

LOVE IN ARIZONA

You are from California,
I am from the Midwest,
But we met in Arizona
And went to the desert
To measure the thorns
Of the lonely, scattered cacti.
We measured the light rays,
Measured the distance
Between us and the world,
Measured the love, kisses, and screams
In the solemn silence of the desert.

We kissed the dusty ground
And asked the dry land for a reason,
But the ground was silent,
And we fell silent, too.
There was no measure, no reason,
Only life, only life
In the desolate desert.
And we kissed more
And did not ask for a reason
Anymore.

RAIN

Those who hate rain hate life.
Nothing reminds us of awakening quite like rain.

We listen to the drops falling
Over the forests, over the rooftops,
Over the streets, and us
As we dream of another unforgettable night
Like this one, which is unrepeatable.
Our emotions flow into the rainy streets,
Soaking the ground even more
With our rainy thoughts and feelings.

As we soar high, we become clouds,
Transforming into drops
That fall over rooftops and streets,
Becoming rain and embracing this feeling.
Little do we know that the rain teaches us
What it means to be alive:
Not knowing, yet still discovering
More than knowledge can ever convey.

Nothing reminds us of awakening quite like rain,
And so we await the sunlight.

MORNING

He placed a rose on the bedside table
While she was still sleeping.
His wake-up message rested on the stand—
Her smile reflected on his face
Filling him with bliss.

Remembrance—
The memory box opens.
Anticipation—
The future is revealed and embraced.

Back and forth,
Through memories and experiences,
She recognizes this morning
In her awakened spirit.

She notices the mist,
The rose, the dewy grass;
She sees his enlightened face
And steps into the new morning with a smile.

THE ART OF LOVE

It was then,

When the breeze tousled your hair,

When you hadn't thought about styling,

Yet were always stylish in your natural grace.

You discovered the source of attraction,

Unaware of the hidden power

Radiating from your face.

You walked confidently

Through the streets of Kotor.

It was then,

When you felt the importance of art,

And realized that without art,

Even love cannot survive—

Love is a unique science.

It was then,

Under the birch tree,

When you felt the breeze

Whispering in your ears,

Conveying untranslatable meanings

That you understood without prior knowledge.

It was then

That you became an artist.

TELL ME EVERYTHING

Sing to me of the times when you first saw the Moon,

When you felt a deep connection with the World,

Understanding more by knowing less,

When you sensed the pulse of the entire family

Hanging in the unknown;

Of the moments when your feelings were innocent;

When a single glance conveyed more than words.

Sing to me about the formation of flowers,

About the shapes of invisible things—

Colors in other dimensions,

About secret formulas;

About feelings you never express in words.

You dream of my life.

I am living your dream—

Writing your book.

Sing to me.

MUSES

MUSE I

Recognize your Muse
Among the multitude of whispers

To see her shining through many colors,
Tune your senses.
Listen to the highest tones.

Fly beyond the scale
To hear her melody,
Adjust your ears and eyes

To colors beyond the spectrum,
Recognize her beyond just yellow and blue,
Creating your own rainbow.

Find a way to connect with her,
Capturing her grace in the sublime
So that the Muse can recognize you

Among the multitudes.
Whisper back to her, using newly invented notes.
Show her the new colors of the rainbow.

MUSE II

Invite me to your Castle;
Arm me with your secret weapons,

To know that I know
What I feel is true;
To know that I feel
What I know is true.

To learn how to lose my senses,
I must make use of the expanding universe
To grow in every direction,
Dream with open eyes and see in the darkness.

I am, and I am not;
You shape me.
You are, and you are not;
We don't truly exist unless we recognize each other.

BIRTHPLACE

My dream is your birthplace;
Your presence is my life.

I follow your spells,
Listen to your songs—
They cure my madness.

You are my savior,
Sending light ahead
So the dream can continue to dream.

Your whispers await me
In every city and street.
The light sings your song.

You save me from myself
During my wanderings.
Those whispers become amulets,

And I keep walking
To keep you alive.

HARBOR

I

I will find you when I least expect it.
You are my Road.

Roads travel through us,
Never arriving at a harbor.

We are both travelers and roads.
All lovers are wanderers.

Our journey is our Road;
Our wanderings are the harbor.

II

You are the Dream,
And I dream of you.

You are the beginning
And the Harbor.

I dream of the world,
And you are the World.

You are here, and you disappear,
Yet you never truly leave me.

You bloom from my heart.
If I lose you, you find me.

If you forget me, I remind you
To dream for me.

If you lose me, I find you
To keep me dreaming.

LIFE

Entering the matter,
You recreate our biology,
Merging with my atoms,
Passing through them like invisible light,

Two swallowing forces—
Not only partners,
But two harmonious songs
Creating new substances.

I am your reason for seeing.
You are my reason for shining.
I am your singer;
You are my song.

You are my ears;
I am your voice.
You are my passion;
I am your measure.

You are my wings;
I am your flight.
You are my life;
I am your dream.

BECOMING ONE

Tell me my story,
And I will tell you yours.

Breathe my air,
And I will be your eyes.

I will hear your whispers
When you translate my touch.

You help me walk,
And I will help you fly.

We will fly and sing,
Circle and fall.

To lift us higher again,
We catch the whispers of flight.

We follow racing words,
Chasing them together.

We see them screaming and making love,
Learning the deepest secrets.

The secret of silence
Draws us into a deep stillness,

Needing nothing—
Not even a word.

THE SAME STORY

Thousands of years old, this story
Tells the same tale we hear today.

We search for new words
To offer new meanings

To old feelings,
Evolving from different sounds

Across time and space
In new landscapes

Where roses smell stronger,
And feelings do not require words.

FANTASY

Life is our fantasy.
We are the actors.

Do we act out life,
Or is life the only true actor?

Do we play our roles,
Or do we attempt to deceive
The greatest Deceiver of all?

Life is the greatest Deceiver's fantasy,
And we are merely actors in his play.

So why do we fantasize about the fantasy?
True fantasy does not require acting.

We shall live it.

THE TOP

I chase you.
You hide—
Then you appear and wave to me.

I chase you again,
Find you by chance,
Then you disappear.

You hit me from behind—
I turn around,
And you are not there.

I chase you once more.
You jump behind the hill
And see me on the peak.

You run into the forest,
Circling and screaming,
Dangerously dancing toward the top.

Then you stop and wait for me—
You kiss me and run away;
The chase doesn't end.

Faster and faster you run;
My legs cannot keep up.
You wear me down.

Then you appear at the top,
Waving to me to join you
So, I slowly step to the top.

"This is where we belong," you said,
And I felt the whole mountain
Tremble for a moment as we hugged.

SIRENS

YOU DON'T NEED TO SAY ANYTHING

What more can we say about voyages,
About the seas, love, loneliness,
Gentle thoughts, tears, and laughter—
What more is there to uncover
About the secrets of the world?

You don't need to say anything;
You need to be, see, and feel—not tell.
The best stories often remain unspoken.
Listening to the sea can open pathways
To the great source of light within you,
As you search for it outside.

For the voyage, you need nothing more
Than a desire to inhale the world.

A NIGHT WORTH A LIFE

I see you anew tonight.
Thoughts on fire,
They burn and scream—
You are new tonight.

Reborn from the fire,
I become a flame,
Burning in bliss
For this brief night.

SPECIAL FEELING

To feel without understanding
And to understand through feeling;
To express it without words
And know it before knowing.

To be silently eloquent
And inquire without asking a question,
To receive the answer nonetheless
And acknowledge it with a smile.

To recognize it through a smile
And express it in silence,
To convey it without actually saying—
That's when you truly understand.

To feel is to know;
Not naming it is to honor it—
To do it for a smile
And not seek any other reward.

To walk, dance, and fly,
Embrace the epiphany of oblivion;
To be one with the world

And live to feel it.

That's when you truly understand it.

UNSAID DELIGHT

What I can say,
And what I cannot say—
It is not just a word,
But an unsaid delight.

What I can sing,
Or only dream—
It is not merely a note,
But an unwritten song.

What I can know
But not express,
Or can express but not fully understand—
It is the moment of greatest intensity.

What I dream,
And do not live—
Or live without dreaming,
Becomes a bad dream.

What I remember,
And what I forget—
It is not merely a memory

But the soul's selective sanctuary.

What I know,
And what I feel,
Even if I can express it in words—
It is a vast unwritten world.

EARLY MORNING

We left early that morning to ride horses,
Feel the fresh air, and see the Sun.
We planned to explore the forest
And rest on a blanket when we grew tired of riding.

We witnessed the red sky
And saw the Sun rising over the forest,
Taking in the refreshing air
In that still, dreamy world.

STAYING CRAZY

I promised to write you a poem
Every day for a year.
Each day, a new flower.
I promised to write flowers for you.

I promised to share a fairy tale
Every day for a year.
I promised something new
And vowed to collect it.

I promised to lift you up—
You were afraid you might fall.
I pledged my words to your throne
To keep the foundation strong.

I promised to write your memory
And rewrite your thoughts.
I promised not to let you fall,
For my words support the throne.

And after every promise delivered,
We became crazier and couldn't believe
How easy it was to keep promises

And how simple it is to be crazy.

As every word became a bird,
And every word blossomed into a flower,
We realized how wonderful it is to be crazy—
And you embraced my madness.

Your fears had no foundation.
You felt comfortable
In your magnificent role.
We promised we would never stop.

We promised never to stop writing poems,
We promised to keep the words soaring,
We promised to keep the throne fresh and alive,
We promised to stay crazy.

YOU ARE THE STAR

Every journey is as ancient and long
As the journey of a star.
You are made of stardust.

Remember your old home,
Your innate glory,
Long travels you've experienced.

There is no place too dark
That cannot be illuminated.
No darkness is stronger than light.

And if you forget—
Or when you forget—
Try to dream and remember.

And if you fall—
Or when you fall—
Remember your home of light.

And if you can't find your way,
Or if you are lost in the jungle,
Look up at the sky.

The sky will guide you on your path.

STAR

Far yet always present,
You were waiting to be born.

From a dream long ago, you emerged,
Waiting to be seen.

Sensed by many but never truly noticed,
Your silent words are understood yet heard by no one.

You touched others, but no one touched you;
You felt sensations while they were asleep.

You needed to be found,
Reborn in an intentional accident.

Though being light, you still needed light,
But no one was a star.

A star needs a star.

TWO STARS

That evening, still alive,
We asked the sea about its secrets
And were surprised it did not hear us,
Or perhaps it was just pretending.

Mediterranean miracles,
The waves of the Adriatic Sea,
Cypresses and mimosas,
Crying insects and fireflies.

Soft like the Mediterranean Sea,
You carried the scent of summer.
You—that evening still alive,
That sea I still see.

The stars were too far and silent.
We screamed to get closer to them,
To break the silence,
To make them hear us.

We were the two loudest creatures
On the entire Mediterranean;
We screamed louder than all the insects and birds,
Imagining we were two stars.

SIREN

From the sea, she sings her seductive song;
Even Odysseus cannot escape it.

Even he falls into her net.
Every man dreams of being ensnared
By a Siren and hearing her song
At least once.

To be captivated
By the enchanting sound of the sea,
And to dream of how to escape
And return to solid ground.

A man proves his courage on the open sea,
Where only the sea measures the sky,
And the sky reflects the sea,
When days are long and nights echo the Siren's song

Of voyages to distant shores,
Every wave hides the secret,
Decodable only through a long friendship with the sky.
Siren was born out of this love.

Every man needs his Siren

To check his courage and strength

When he hears her song

In his travels through the unknown.

DREAMS

DON QUIXOTE

We dream and fight
With demons, both real and imagined
We truly live only when we dream;
We grow from our dreams,

From our own La Mancha.
Don Quixote is not merely an imaginary figure;
He is as real as Alexander the Great,
His Dulcinea is as real as Cleopatra.

His windmills are as real as the Library of Alexandria;
As real as the many languages that are now dead and forgotten;
As real as Attila or the loss of Constantinople.
His windmills represent lost Ayah Sofias,

His battles had to be fought
By sleepy emperors
Too preoccupied to engage in them.
We need Don Quixote and La Mancha

For when the whole past feels like a phantom,
When many cities have fallen,
The idea remains—

Stronger than any city, stronger than any empire.

Quixote shines through Lorca and Picasso;
From Dalí and El Greco;
From the gloomy *View of Toledo.*
He was born before Cervantes.

Those in Argentina, Mexico, and Peru,
Colombia and the Caribbean
Carry La Mancha and Quixote in their hearts,
For he is an ultimate and often overlooked Don Juan.

Garcia Márquez was not born in Colombia.
He was born in Macondo,
And his Macondo is his La Mancha.
Fuentes and Cortázar are from La Mancha, too.

Neruda had his first dream,
First meeting with the Moon and the Sun,
In sunny La Mancha, hiding in his heart,
Where he learned how to sing like a nightingale.

Don Quixote is not just Don Quixote;
La Mancha is not just geography.
It is our inner territory—
Terra Nostra.

It does not matter what happens where,

Where we fall or rise,

What we conquer or lose,

How big or small we are.

All places come and go.

History will be erased in the universal purgatory.

Dreams are our only geography—

Our native land.

THE WORLD

Fight against those who oppose beauty,
And share what you observe
When you interpret the words of light—
The essence of all worlds.

The same story exists across all worlds,
Yet each world is distinct,
Just as every word offers new meaning
To the universal Source of Everything.

WE COME FROM THE SAME PLACE

You say we come from the same place.

You claim that you have lived within me since we parted ways

And that I have lived within you.

We are each other's home, and that is where we belong.

HEART

Deceived by feelings and misled by knowledge—
You should turn to the heart,
Or allow the mind to calculate and deceive you even further.

Do you hear the music of the heart when you listen to it?
Let it guide your choices, and do not regret it.

DON JUAN

The most charming psychopath in history,
Whether real or imagined,
Played with the dreams of women
Who believed he would be gentle
And wouldn't betray love.

By recognizing their dreams,
He seduced them into the game
Of playing out their own stories,
Uncovering the secrets of their hearts
In the seductive hell of deceit.

LOVER

There is no born lover,
For we are all lovers

Although some are in a state of amnesia,
Overlooking the light of a sleeping star.

To dream occasionally is not dreaming
To love occasionally is not love.

There is always a dreaming star
Hiding within you, waiting to shine.

LIVE TO LOVE

To truly live,
To live for love,
To love for love,
To be alive,

We don't need devices
As much as we need scents.
We don't need more air
As much as we need new wings.

We don't need new elements—
We need refreshment.
Nothing is ever new;
It is only a discovery.

We need to desire to fly,
To fly to live,
To fly to love,
To love flying and to live flying.

RECIPE FOR LOVE

If someone needs lessons in love,
They may already be lost.
From ashes, you cannot ignite a fire;
Perhaps they are souls that have already burned out.

But, maybe they can learn how not to hate—
How to appreciate the closeness
Of someone who does not require a teacher,
And how to understand rather than just learn.

It's as simple as walking, talking, eating, or breathing,
Yet for some people, it seems harder than building a house.
However, what is the value of a house
Without these invisible ingredients built into it?

ARMOR OF LOVE

Love will save you from despair,

Of a certain death—

Death cannot outsmart love.

It is your armor,

Protecting you from the tricks of life.

CHANCES

FIRST LOVE

Forgotten feelings and words,
Or are we simply asleep?

Shy to feel or too weak to name it,
Afraid of losing or being lost and frozen

In a hug, while the music played,
On the terrace in St. Stefan

When we first felt it
And watched the mischievous waves

Drumming like a pendulum
Against the shore.

MOMENTS WORTH THE WHOLE ETERNITY

They happen anytime,
In any place,
In ways we don't understand.
We only know they are true.

When we ask for a reason,
We know they are not real.
When we cannot find the answer,
We know they are true.

We see more light,
Becoming lighter,
Knowing they are
Moments worth an eternity.

I throw a little dagger;
It flies back to me
And wounds me more deeply.
That is the price we pay.

When we say hello,
It is done with a smile,
And when we say goodbye,
It is with a kiss.

FLOWER

You are more than you realize.
A flower doesn't recognize its fragrance.

The One who unfolds your petals
Holds the key to your soul.

From the shimmering source, you shine from within,
And deep inside, he senses that source.

PATH

You either find the Path,
Or the Path finds you.

If the Path makes a choice,
You will become the light.

When there is no light,
You will still see.

When the light is too bright,
You will not be blinded.

You will be neither lost in darkness
Nor seduced by glory.

The light is your birthplace;
Life is your Path.

THE HEALING POWER OF A KISS

A kiss in the morning
Is enough to start the day.

A kiss at dawn
Is enough to begin a whole life.

A kiss in every place—
Under the tree, on the sidewalk,

On the bridge, and along both shores.
In our wanderings, it serves as a talisman.

A kiss in your memory is an instant delight
When you feel sad and alone.

FUN

Tell me a joke so we can laugh together.
We might even defy the law of gravity
By creating a new law of gravity
Filled with joy and adventure,
Ensuring lifelong fun.

WORDS AND LEAVES

Words and music fill the air—
Leaves dance on a windy day,
Waiting for a passerby,
A fleeting moment to embrace
And catch its melody,
Fading slowly into oblivion.

UNFORESEEN MOMENT

Something always lingers,

Forgotten deeply and unresolved,

Waiting to return at an unforeseen moment,

Reminding us to accept it as due.

BREAK UP

It ended.
Just like that—
Quick,
No explanation.

Are all problems so simple?
Or do they linger, dying a slow, overdue death
Under the weight of reasoning?

With poor explanations,
Poor judgments,
And poorer decisions.

It is better this way—
Quick,
As sharp as a knife.
A new opportunity

For life awaits
For another chance,
And for you.

THE LILAC LAND

LILAC WORLD

Words have their own fragrances,
And can transform the world into a garden of flowers.
Every petal carries a new word, a new scent.

The world becomes a giant lilac.
"Breathe me," I say.
We have been waiting for a long time,
Both in a rush and at leisure.

Amid the turmoil, you whispered,
"You might miss your chances."
You reminded me
That we should not pursue every opportunity before us;
An obvious opportunity can be a distraction,
Preventing us from seeing the bigger chance ahead.

You taught me that
Sometimes, the best opportunities are the ones we choose not to act
    upon.
The greatest successes can come unexpectedly,
And the best chances arise from patience.

Neither of us hit the first ball.

Neither of us seized every opportunity.

Our score reflects the missed opportunities and chances.

We chose not to take every chance

By refraining from pursuing every opportunity that came our way.

The breeze carries our whispers

As we dance and savor them under the starry sky

In the lilac world, where we arrived by passing up another chance.

WORDS, MUSIC, AND LIGHT
I

Words cannot heal the deep wounds caused by impatience.

Healing comes from understanding those wounds,
Rooted in the pain of birth and the struggles of growth.

Words become ineffective when perspective is limited.
They cannot mend a soul another has hurt,

Nor can they bridge the gap
Created by unseen vistas and unheard sounds.

Everything is a word, but it is more than just a word.
Light sings, and music shines.

II

Words are sources of both sorrow and joy,

Soft and sharp, like swords,

Carrying fragrances

Filled with the sounds of singing birds,

Whispers, and flowing rivers.

The world emerges from words.

Words guide our roles and actions.

We strive to conquer and enchant one another

To win the ultimate game,

Navigating unpredictable paths,

Becoming both servants and rulers.

Yet, we drift apart.

Countless words build walls between us,

Sucking up the air and destroying bridges,

Leaving no room for movement;

No space for words,

And no chance to mend anything.

All words can be lethal—both soft and sharp;

To soothe our pride, we let them take control.

Excessive knowledge can extinguish love,

As we learn to live beyond words and grow from silence.

III

Words are flying
From the leaves,
And we are trying to catch them.

You are soaring with them,
Catching them mid-flight
And bringing them to me.

You attempt to build a garden,
Enchanting whispers
Singing about the journey.

Every lily holds your secret:
A new whisper, a new word, a new flower.
We are getting closer to the Garden.

Nobody knows
About our secret palace;
Nobody senses its existence.

I am landing in your Garden,
You take me by the hand,
Turning another page into a lily.

The scents are flowing;
Every page reveals a new flower.
I am moving through your Castle.

Every room holds a new word,
New flowers blooming,
New whispers and scents.

I am moving through your Castle,
Where every sound sings,
And every word has a smell.

Then, I find the most comfortable corner
Of your Castle and lie on your pillows,
Feeling your touch.

And you move into my heart,
Savoring my words.
"This is your Castle," you say.

IV

Letters grow on the trees,
Rivers flow towards us.
The world expands from us.
We hear more and say less,
Or speak only what we must.
We need no measurements
For actions that seek no recognition.
The world is clear, and we are clear.

V

You give life to my words
That brush against me through your lips,
And my lips echo your kisses.
We understand our silence,
And we deserve it.

THE LIGHT OF THE MIND

A STAR IN THE MIND
INNER SPACE

A STAR DEEP IN THE MIND

I see a new star on the horizon.

It's not a Morning Star;

It's a star without light.

The star without light is the brightest,

But its glow remains within.

The star without light is the largest,

But it doesn't occupy any space.

It exists within itself.

It nourishes all other stars

And the entire physical World.

Without space, there is no time.

Without time, there is no aging.

Without aging, there is no death.

The star without light never dies.

It cannot be seen in outer space,

But it can be sensed deep within the mind.

ISLAND

Dreams, flying out from the mind,
Become birds flying over the sea.

The Sun, sprouting from the sea,
Makes the sea blue.

The flying dream that hovers in space
Becomes an Island in the sea.

The Island—the dream from the mind,
The bird, the air, the sea, and the light.

INNER SPACE

To become a flying saucer,

Entering a cell and penetrating deep,

To find a new galaxy

Would be an honorable task

For a new scientist

More interested in the inner state

Of the soul than in outer space.

THE SOURCE

There exists a substance

Beyond mere materiality,

A mind that transcends physical matter.

It grows from within,

Follows its own path,

Nourished solely by the desire to live.

This is how matter is born,

How the first poet sings

The shamanic song,

How he romantically

Engages with nothingness

Using the flower of the mind,

Emerging from the Universal Source

Of Everything.

AFTERLIFE LIGHT

It is no longer present,

But we can still see it,

And you will see it

For millions of years to come.

Did the Star die? Did it live?

In life, we call this phenomenon

A ghost, a hallucination.

(Is life a ghost?)

What if the star never lived at all?

Or maybe death dies

While the star continues to live,

Cheating on death

With the afterlife light.

THE LIGHT FROM THE MIND

Morning fills the mind with light,

Inviting the world

On a journey through uncharted territory,

Where daisies awaken slowly and thrive longer

Thanks to spring's arrival in the desert.

In this garden stands a temple,

Bathed in the glow of light from within,

Opening a long path through the desert

For the world to discover its way

To land safely in your thoughts,

Glowing with a faithful light.

SEAGULL FROM FAR

Lie down on the ground and listen to the grass,

Soar high to catch the quiet signals

Of music from outer space,

Dream by creating and create by dreaming.

Become the thing you observe,

Feel what the trees, bathed in sunlight, experience.

Breathe in the world, not just the air.

Gaze far into the distance to see

The seagull emerging from the sea.

Imagine it as the birth of the world and greet it.

Welcome the old bird

That has flown from afar to meet you.

Fulfill your desire to fly, see, and be seen.

MEMORY AND OBLIVION

When everything is lost, there remains a memory
From which a new city will be built, a new world.
Those who have memory will be rich.

Oblivion heals old wounds; you must agree.
On the road, there is only the past and the future.
When everything is lost, there remains a memory.

Memory will save oblivion from bad dreams.
When the new city is built, it will become a temple bestowed
By those who have memory to make others wealthy.

In the center of the city, before the temple,
The keepers of the fire will all abide.
When everything is lost, there remains a memory.

From night, fire will be born
As new light when all knowledge is swallowed.
Those who have memory will be rich.

A new rose will bloom from the dark sea,
A city revived from memory and abode.
When all is but a memory, there remains a memory.
Those who have memory will be rich.

I REMEMBER THE SNOW IN THE SUMMER'S LIGHT

I remember the snow in the summer's light,
Thinking of summer in winter and of winter in summer.
When I see the blue, I know the white.

I see the haze over the rooftops bright
And feel the warm air caressed by the azure.
I remember the snow in the summer's light.

Summers were lazy in my inner sight;
Winters, lazy on the outside, were sure to secure
The blue when I felt the cold of the white.

Winter takes me on summer's flight
To visit the summer and to endure
The snows while remembering the light.

Maybe I like spring and fall the most,
But winter becomes spring in the summer to allure.
I feel the fall and see the blue in the white.

I keep remembering, seeing all bright—
Everything is just a thought you conjure.
I remember the snow hiding in the light;
When I see the blue, I know the white.

DON'T OBSTRUCT THE SUN

"Don't obstruct the Sun,"
Said Diogenes to the great man.
Even great men respect the wishes
Of those indifferent to power,
But close to the source,
Without whose help
Great men would blindly
Sit in darkness.
Even the great men bow before the Sun,
Which melts hubris into humility,
Making a human more human.

THE NEW SUN AND THE NEW MOON

EMBRACING A NEW DAY

Finding a way, when it seems there is none,

Feels impossible. Yet the world

Changes its appearance from time to time,

Following the trends of the moment.

It flirts with VIPs of all kinds:

Entrepreneurs, politicians,

Professors, scientists, and authors—

So-called famous people of every type.

While everything changes,

Some things remain constant,

The familiar world appears anew.

NEW HOME

She followed her thoughts,
Nourished by her dreams,
Unaware of her own self-realization,
Yet she understood the power of desire,
As it emerged from her dreams and transformed
Into clear thoughts and visions
Of what awaits her if she stays focused.
She knew that something was waiting,
Ready to embrace her dreams far ahead,
Once her thoughts demonstrated
Devotion and loyalty to those dreams.

It was the smiling dreams
That had been waiting for her all along.

A NEW FRIEND

Tell me something less significant—

Something about our biology, for example,

About unjustified failures,

Rather than fame and success.

Tell me what you hear while sitting under the tree,

Or share stories of lonely lions in the prairies.

Forget about decorated generals;

Tell me about Private Ryan instead.

Share something only you know,

And make a new friend.

THE NEW SUN AND THE NEW MOON

Too much has already been written

About the Sun and the Moon.

We have started to believe that both of them

Have somehow become new.

However, the Sun remains the same old Sun,

And the Moon is still the same old Moon.

While many things have changed

Among human beings and their affairs,

The Sun and the Moon have stayed the same.

THE SEA AND THE WORLD

The sea, the music, the morning.
While the world sleeps, the sea sings
Quietly about the path the world takes.
It sings from the depths, sending signals
For the world to find its way,
Spreading the scent of its mystery—
A song about its own enigma,
Reflecting on the meaning of shores,
Waiting for the world to arrive safely
In the harbor of silence.

THE WORLD IS NEITHER HAPPY NOR SAD

The world has suddenly become sad.

There is too much cheering,

Too much unsubstantiated hope.

Who would claim that

Everything could change overnight?

Hopes are merely dreams,

Evaporating much faster

Than they are built.

And we stand hypnotized,

Paralyzed by this sudden revelation,

Accusing the world and blaming our hopes,

Hoping to find another excuse

For yet another episode

Of postponed endings—

Of something that should have ceased long ago.

Even hopes have their limits.

In this new episode,

Actors must confront themselves

Instead of living in a dreamland.

The world remains neither sad nor happy.

INDIFFERENT WORLD

I struggle with words,
With visions, ideas, and imagination.
There is too much competition
Among them, and too little time
To experience them all, to see them all
Come to life in an indifferent world,
Equally indifferent to their existence.

LITTLE WORLD

Let's forget about important things today.

Let's focus on little things and use simple words.

For instance, let's sit in the garden.

Let's forget crowds and let go of our goals.

Let us become the goals we are trying to achieve.

Let us be small in a big world

And see if the world welcomes

Our desire to simply exist

Without too much pomp or pretension.

NEW WORLD

People talk about a New World Order,

But what if we could create a New World instead?

We need new horizons, not just cover-ups,

Not the same old system dressed up as new.

New horizons can inspire proper governance,

Fostering innovation and a just approach,

Creating fresh partnerships and opportunities.

This shift could mean fewer wars;

Even if it doesn't cultivate more love,

It could spark greater compassion,

Illuminating the path of awakened souls

To build a New Temple as a lighthouse,

Spreading light instead of darkness

Over the tiny planet we call home.

The New World represents a new way of thinking,

As opposed to the New World Order,

Which is rooted in outdated beliefs

That serve as a facade created by detached politicians,

Manipulative individuals, and greedy entrepreneurs

Who lament the little space left in their pockets

To stow away more corporations.

The world is weary of the old order,

Which changes names to favor a select few.

Let's forget history for a moment and focus on the present,

On the notions of imposed order.

Imagine a place where goodness prevails—

An Island of Hope in the desert of despair,

Where all hands and minds unite with shared goals.

BRIGHT MOMENTS

BRIGHT MOMENTS

There can be no forced inspiration,
But there can be mergers with the world,

There can be a flow of feelings,
Yet it can be overwhelming,

Flying outside to unite,
Flying inside to find

The melody of the moment,
When the yellow corona appears on the horizon

And another one across the mountain,
When the world turns mellow,

Hospitable and generous,
And you fly into the heart of the mountain

To find the egg of an unborn bird,
To break free and soar like a newborn eagle.

THIS IS SO SIMPLE

I sense the light within and around me.
The Sun is close and keen.

The world glows and I glow,
The world is expanding.

And I grow glowing,
Believing this is quite simple,

Not to think, but to glisten
Not to understand, but to feel

The light inside and outside
And grow by shining.

UNENDING LIFE

People often contemplate life after life.

Perhaps they believe there was no life before life,

Or perhaps they don't care about life before life.

Yet, if there were life before life,

There must be life beyond life.

If we existed before our birth,

We will be here even after we die.

But if there was no individuality before,

Why would it exist afterward?

It appears that this is not a matter of life

Or death, but a problem of ego

That does not accept the disappearance

Of individuality within the sea

Of an unending life for all.

AN OLD WOMAN

She relished fresh figs in the summer,

Gazing at their green skin,

Gently opening them

To savor the pink interior

Before consuming them.

During winter,

She savored dried figs and smoked fish,

Savoring them slowly

As if she learned it

From a Buddhist monk

On small joys.

Observing these rituals was enjoyable.

Not exactly eating

As for taking the necessary time.

POETRY AND LIFE

"Why poetry?" you ask.
Because of life, I respond.

Why love? Why hate? Why destruction?
Everything has a reason behind it.

The question of why always remains,
But there is a life that craves to be lived.

The answer to life is to live it,
And life itself does not require an answer.

TOO MUCH THINKING

His problem was that he was a deep thinker.

Excessive thinking can lead to paralysis.

While it inspires imagination,

Sometimes wild imagination

Loses touch with reality, creating projections

Of unimaginable and impossible desires.

This can feed the ego, causing it to grow too quickly,

Moving far ahead of its own steps

And straying from the path toward what is real.

It can often feel like arriving either too soon or too late.

Yet another question arises: do we truly know or understand

What is real or unreal, and what is too soon or too late?

NOES

When people want to be polite, they say, yes.
It is easy to reach an agreement while having fun.
And the same person who often says yes,
Often responds negatively when doing business.
Wit does not lead to approval.

WHO KILLED BEAUTY

You killed it!

How can I be sure?
I assisted you.
But now I feel ashamed,
Prepared for prosecution,
Ready to endure all consequences.
I want beauty back,
And you are cowards
For not admitting the crime.

HELL FROM THE HEART

Dark thoughts, dark images,
I cast spells on you.

I prefer to live with cheap sunsets
Rather than the rich descriptions of Hell!

Go away, dark thoughts,
Dark images, dark words,

Smuggled into the world
By the messengers of despair.

Go away, Hell!
I cast a spell on all of you.

If you return,
I will not rely solely on spells.

TOP OF THE MOUNTAIN IN THE MIDDLE OF THE STREET

THE
Summit
Seemed distant,
Yet it felt close and ordinary.
We loved visiting the mountains
But feared falling from the high cliffs.
These were not large mountains like Kilimanjaro,
But smaller ones filled with grass, spring flowers, and trees.
We attempted to ascend to the top and look down at the valley
And the city below, feeling as if we had reached the sky when we
stood
At the summit of the conquered Blue Mountain. However, we had
To make our way back down slowly and carefully to return
To the world in the valley and the bustling city,
More afraid of falling as we jumped down.
Some of us crawled to ensure a safe
Descent. We worried about those
Who seemed uncertain in their
MOVEMENT.

At one point, I fell from a small cliff and landed directly in the city street, surrounded by cars, hurried passengers, and pedestrians rushing as if they were trying to reach the top of the mountain I had just conquered. I fell back into the chaos of the busy world, feeling even more frightened after safely returning to the midst of it all.

CLEPSYDRA

I

what if a human civilization existed for about a million years,

or even one hundred million? What if there were only one

Homer every thousand years, one Dante in another

Thousand, and one Shakespeare in yet another?

That would amount to one thousand

Notable figures in a million years,

Or one hundred thousand

In one hundred million

Years. Who would

Be able to read

ALL

Of them

In a single lifetime,

Unless life were to be

Significantly extended in the future?

Perhaps there are civilizations like this

Scattered throughout the Universe, where beings

Can access the memories of their entire species. If we are

Fortunate, ours might become one of them. In such a scenario,

exceptional individuals like Homer, Dante, and Shakespeare could

Become more common and, as a result, might not receive the same

level of recognition they do now.

II

Perhaps this civilization would discover a way to condense and

Express ten or even one hundred times more thought in ten

Or one hundred times fewer words than we do now.

Or perhaps we would all become similar in

Knowledge but differ in desires, allowing

Us to avoid boredom as time progresses.

When the moment comes to navigate

This brief passage

And transition

INTO

A new realm of thinking

And understanding regarding

The human condition in the entire

Universe, or just on one planet, there might

Be an opportunity to construct a new temple, a new

Library in the heart of the Galaxy, perhaps even within

A black hole. This library could house the knowledge of

Angels or higher beings, and we might even enter a larger

Universe where our own is merely a minor planet or atom.

FEELINGS AND THOUGHTS

BEAUTY

It is beautiful to talk about beautiful things,
And even more beautiful to silently gaze at them.

It is beautiful to express love,
And even more beautiful to feel it.

Beauty is a cheap word
But beauty remains priceless.

UNUSUAL LOVE

You accepted my dreams, but I'm unsure if you accepted my
 thoughts.
You accepted conversations, but I'm unsure if you accepted ideas.
You accepted the words, but I'm unsure you understood the
 meanings.

This came long after the first hello,
Long after the turbulence of rough rides,
Long after accommodations and adjustments.

I have learned to accept your unusual ways,
Your intriguing thoughts on life, dreams, and the interplay between
 them.
I learned to accept your typical ways of expressing unusual desires.

Desires soared like birds in the morning,
When we are woken by the chimes of dreams,
Hypnotized and prepared for another round of living.

We would stroll down the street of a foreign city, mesmerized
By its history, recognized in the streets and gardens,
Filled with exotic flowers and grass—you loved the grass.

You loved green and blue.

You loved leaping into the water from the cliffs.

I have always felt afraid when you did that.

You mentioned you would teach me everything.

I never really found out what it was, but I agreed to be your

    student,

To learn whatever it may be.

You loved my mind and my words.

Other than that, you thought I could be complicated.

I have always known that nothing is easy

And accepted the ways of life, your uniquely typical ways,

And I lived a life I never thought I would.

It felt like a typhoon sweeping through paradise.

I thought I knew you

Although I can hardly see if I even knew myself.

That's how life often works.

What about psychology?

There is no way to analyze how a brain machine works,

The function of billions of cells, transmitters, and neurons

Flying, fighting, and competing.

How do ideas become reality?

That was yet another tricky question.

I could not find out anything about anything,

Except that I was alive and felt alive, yet I also felt dead;

I watched the rain, the fog, the horses, the birds, the trees, and the
blue.

I enjoyed watching the blue every day.

You loved the same, though perhaps for different reasons;

Perhaps we loved each other for different reasons as well.

Did we hate each other?

I'm not sure. There were a few times when I felt hate towards you.

Did you hate me? Perhaps you did at times.

And perhaps you still hate me,

When you think of that July when blue was everywhere,

With the white dot in the middle shining like it was the first time,

When everything was lush,

And you were glistening at the center of it all—the blue, the green,
the summer,

But I was not there for either love or hate.

FEELINGS AND THOUGHTS

Love flows abundantly within me.

I feel as if I might explode.

Then, "love less or open the window,"

Said the whisper in my mind or in the air.

YOU WILL NEVER LEAVE

No, you shall not leave.
You will remain here to dream with me.

No, you will not be leaving.
You will remain here to build a new home,

And even if you must leave,
You will always return home.

THE END OF THE PARTY

When she entered the room, she sensed trouble,
Although everything appeared to be in order.
The music played while people talked.
It was an ordinary party.
She stayed in the corner for a while, watching silently,
Pondering that strange feeling.
A man entered the room, walking past her,
Moving to the center of the room
Where there was a beautiful face with long blond hair
Shining above all the rest, giggling and
Talking. Bang, bang (she heard in the air).

That marked the end of the party.

WE WILL UNDERSTAND ONE ANOTHER

When those who traveled far return
And those who have never left begin to leave,
When memories are shared and understood,
We will understand each other.

When people with big ideas move to the corner,
And those in the corner move closer to the center.
When ideas are shared and comprehended,
Perhaps we will understand one another.

GOD AND LOVE

There are many unwritten histories and numerous religions,
But people usually adhere to just one.
According to monotheistic beliefs, there is only one God,
Yet numerous different texts exist about that same God.
We often prioritize the scriptures of our heritage
Over the universal God who serves all,
Regardless of our backgrounds and the poor choices
Made by fickle human beings.

There are different types of love,
And who can truly explain the major differences between them?
Countless lives have been lost
Over ideas about love and relationships,
But we often forget that the most important thing
Is to live and love.
Without living, life is worthless,
And love without living is lifeless.

There is life and there is existence.
The availability of love seems to be diminishing,
Regardless of the love offered from all directions.
Too many words attempt to replace the strong feelings

That were once felt most intensely in silence.

You once found happiness in that silence,

Even without fully understanding

Your emotions; it simply felt good.

There is everything and there is nothing.

When you love, everything exists,

And everything feels present.

In the absence of love,

There is a profound emptiness that fills your heart.

If you hate, everything feels dead,

And the entire world transforms

Into one immense void.

There are many religions,

But for the majority of believers, God is one.

There are many loves and many love stories,

But love is love, regardless of different experiences.

The only God worth believing in is the God of Love.

If there is a God, it must be Love.

The God of Love is Love itself.

If it is not Love God is not God.

Love is God and God is Love.

INSIDE AND OUTSIDE

It's difficult to be simple
When everything around is grand.
It's difficult to understand
When everything appears to be a mystery,
To love from a great distance,
To see inside while staying outside,
To pop a balloon, if that is all there is,
To discover a vast blue sky within,
To fly as far as your wings allow,
And dream that everything is much simpler
Than it appears from the outside.

UNPRETENTIOUS DREAMS

How difficult is it to refrain

From saying too much?

How difficult is it to love more—

To express simple ideas,

To live like a river gently eroding the stone,

To observe the distant spot from the shore,

To imagine places basking in its light,

Observe not just colors, shapes, or the sea,

But the simple life glistening

And hovering like a bird,

Filled with unpretentious dreams,

Satisfied solely with the ability to fly.

DO NOT COMPETE WITH THE SUN

Prune, but do not over-prune.

Shine, but don't compete with the Sun.

Beauty is indifferent to our desires.

It is as precise as a mathematical formula.

Don't strive to be an artist,

Be someone who embodies experience and trust.

Your concerns are often unfounded.

They originate from your ego, not from reality.

ADVICE FROM AN OLD MAN

Try not to be overly clever, and everything could turn out well.

Everything can be put in words, but not truly expressed.

There is beauty in words, but even more in hidden ones.

Love, scream, cry, hate, but never overkill.

Don't tell me you love me, make me believe you.

Don't say too much, but don't say too little either.

Balance is dictated more by sincerity than by craftsmanship.

I don't believe in prominent names; I only believe in facts.

When you find yourself, knock on my door.

If you wander too often, try to stay still for a moment.

Don't consider yourself too important, because you are not.

Don't fight for a place in history; fight for your place in life.

Don't tell me stories; pull me into the story and be a good host.

Don't try to seduce me with words; seduce me with their interplays
and happenings.

SILENT EQUALITY

BEST INTENTIONS

She bid a quick goodbye.
He stood there, speechless,
Frozen for a moment and taken aback,
Even though he had the best intentions
And hadn't done anything wrong.

AN IDEA

I cannot find the drawer

Where an old idea is preserved

In the universe of my mind.

Perhaps I never had an idea at all,

But only the concept of a concept—

A spark that suddenly ignited,

Or a memory of something

That never existed.

LATE WISDOM

I need to change my life,
But first, I must change myself,
And for that, it is too late.

FLYING AND MEDITATION

Meditation is beneficial occasionally,
But flying every day is even better.

MOUNTAINS AND SEAS

Mountains and seas
You exist within me

When I climb
To the top

Of the mind
Or dive deep

To the bottom
Of the heart

THE RETURN

I visited many exotic places,

Some very far away,

But I always returned to myself.

WONDER

Every day,
I wander and wonder
How peculiar
Everything around me seems.
It's strange to think
That I exist among it all,
Observing, inhaling its scent,
Hearing, touching,
Tasting, and feeling it
Every day.

STUPIDITY

When I want to remind myself of foolishness,
Especially my own, I switch on the TV.

BABY SQUIRREL

It walked in front of me on the sidewalk,
Barely the size of a mouse.
What are you doing here, poor little squirrel?
I watched it, fearing for its safety.

How did you get lost among people?
Far from the safety of your grassy home?
What was your mother doing?
Will anyone ever hold her accountable for neglecting you?

The squirrel shifted to the left,
Toward the entrance of a building, but the door was closed.
Then, it did what I feared—
It shifted to the right and found itself on the street.

As it reached the midpoint of the road,
Cars zoomed past. It attempted to turn back,
But I heard and saw nothing
Except for an SUV speeding by and other vehicles.

I believed it had a chance to return,
But time passed, and I could no longer see the little squirrel.

I returned to the street but found only

A tiny red mark on the pavement.

SILENT EQUALITY

It is impossible to say more than what is possible.

Unjustified ambition kills value and eats its own life,

Destroys another person's desire to soar,

Cuts their wings, and sucks in the air.

Get out, but avoid causing unnecessary accidents.

Nearly all of us believe we are clever,

And we all believe we are important,

But there is only so much space, only so much time,

Only so much desire, only as many words,

As few pages as possible, as little ink as necessary,

To accept all of us at light speed,

Hurrying into the Promised Land

Of oblivion, waiting for us sooner or later.

There is no reason for such a feverish rush,

For we shall arrive at the same place.

Justice will be served at the right time.

There will be neither better nor worse,

No distinctions between big and small,

No rewards, no punishment,

No guilt, no judgment, no hierarchies,

Only a silent equality.

SECRET OF LIFE

Perhaps the secret of life

Lies in not being too easy or too good,

To achieve the purpose effortlessly.

The purpose is always fleeting.

It is always the goal, almost equally distant

From when we started toward it.

Yet, there is always an invisible progression,

Slow and challenging to recognize;

It remains steady if we do not give in to weakness.

There is no perfect balance,

And within this imbalance lies the equilibrium

Of our efforts and achievements toward that purpose.

We call this pursuit the meaning of life.

While it can be challenging,

It may seem easier for those unwilling to fight for anything.

Success requires a willingness to pay the price.

BIG DREAMS

A MAN AND THE SEA: HOMAGE TO HEMINGWAY

It murmurs tirelessly, a forgotten song,

Telling the same story in the same way.

It listens to itself, indifferent to you,

Yet it charms and envelops you

With its music coming from afar.

It lulls you to sleep and then wakes you

With the same song, never tired

Of repeating its melody.

You go to the sea

To listen every morning,

Standing alone on the shore,

Inhaling the fresh scent

Of the ever-young and inviting world,

Happy to see you and greet you every time.

TEACHERS

We often disdain clichés,

Yet we pay a heavy price for them.

On television, in the streets,

In the Senate and classrooms,

Even in poetry,

Every word seems to be a cliché.

Neologisms aren't celebrated

Unless we view slang

As a new form of language.

Perhaps uniqueness

Resides in new combinations

Or in ordinary speech,

Transformed by extraordinary training

From a workshop

Led by an everyday enthusiast

Who, we must concede,

Has a profound love

For something that generates income,

Which supports a livelihood,

Even at the expense of what it is meant to teach.

LAZARONE

A wanderer through the streets, aimless and free,
No destination torments his soul.
Sometimes, while sitting on the curb, he becomes lost in thought.
At other times, he stands, watching the chaotic world.

A few coins fall softly from time to time.
There is no understanding between him and those around him.
To them, he's a disgrace, a shadow on their path,
While he sees them as lost souls chasing echoes.

In his reality, there is no journey from A to B,
Yet theirs is confined, wrapped tightly in routine.
He lacks freedom too, but wonders—can they not see?
Their chains are invisible, yet ever so present.

They call him a beggar; he views them with jest—
Professionals, each one, selling pieces of their lives.
To him, their labor is merely well-disguised stress,
While he embraces the art of simply being alive.

They think him a fool, a mere drifter in the dark,
But he carries a philosopher's heart within.

He knows that Diogenes would face similar scorn

If he wandered today beneath the same Sun's spin.

In cities like Rome or bustling New York,

They would cast their eyes down, seeing only the rags,

Missing the wisdom cloaked in simplicity,

Blind to the thoughts that dance beneath the labels.

So he carries on, a silent observer,

Finding beauty in moments most would dismiss.

In a world that rushes, he savors the still,

A question mark longing for answers in bliss.

EGOCENTRIC

How beautiful I am.

How grand my ideas are!

What I have accomplished and what I will achieve—

And what else could I do, if only they knew.

But he never understood who he referred to as "they."

He never realized that others could see

If there is beauty anywhere else—

If only he were aware.

BEAUTIFUL WORDS AND VANITY

I enjoy using beautiful words to express lovely thoughts,
Yet true beauty doesn't rely solely on elegant language,
Nor can it be conveyed entirely by it.
Often, it cries out for recognition in the somber corners of our
    minds.

Complicated words and complex ideas—
Illusions that spring from selfish dreams—
Eager to be acknowledged and celebrated,
Welcomed as profound insights rather than mere daydreams.

What sustains these illusions is nothing more than vanity.

PLACE OF BIRTH

Some believe they emerge from specific soil,
Others find their roots
Wrapped in the arms of a nation,
While some are encircled by kin or community.
Yet, some drift, untethered,
Without land, without lineage,
And without a name to call their own.

Every place can feel like a cage,
Every boundary is a chain—
Limiting the desire to stretch and soar.
But when you find your home
In every corner of the earth,
And every horizon feels familiar,
You come to realize:

There is no single territory,
No solitary tribe or nation
That can define your essence.
Instead, the world unfolds
As your cradle, your birthplace,
Where every heart beats
In rhythm with the universe.

In that vast embrace, you discover—

The whole world is your singular place of birth.

PERFECT BOREDOM

When there is noise and a crowd, trouble follows.

When everything is silent and perfect, it feels complete,

Yet there is nothing to fill the air but boredom.

BIG DREAMS

Much has already been said about many topics,

Yet our desire to express ourselves continues to grow.

What can we really say about this?

Speaking isn't always just about talking,

Growth isn't defined solely by progress,

And a strong desire alone isn't enough

To meet the expectations tied to unfulfilled dreams.

A PRAYER

Come to me, words,
Come to me, thoughts,
Come to me, songs,
I pray for your presence every day.

DEATH

Death is not death.

(At least not in a way people perceive it.)

If birth is a manifestation of life,

Then death is another manifestation.

Why concern ourselves with death?

Why pay more attention to death than to birth?

Just accept it without overthinking,

While living in the meantime.

Every thought about death

Takes away a moment of life.

LIFE IS POETRY

IMPERFECTION

Trying too hard to be too good,
Even when attempting to be bad,
It turns out too good for the bad,
And too bad for the good.

Perfection is often desired,
But it can feel sterile—
Final, with no mystery in it,
Like a product from an assembly line.

We wish for perfection,
Yet perfection is unachievable.
To attain perfect perfection,
A little touch of imperfection helps.

JUDGES AND ART

We don't have control over words;
This battle is already lost.
We can only use leftovers,
Assembling crumbs into music.
We think that clever arrangements
Are enough to create harmony.
We believe that a few lessons in prosody,
A decent knowledge of exotic words,
And some techniques for organizing everything
Are sufficient to make it seem
As if it comes from sincere inspiration and experience.
We assume this is enough to create real art,
Yet these artificial cacophonies,
Assembled as if they were symphonies,
Consist of words put together simply to be together—
Only because they sound good together
Or convey a certain idea about a supposed feeling.
Such works often attract the attention of judges,
Who serve as instant critics or measures
To assess the value of a product
Crafted to sound pleasant and convincing
Enough to be called art.
And for many, that is enough
To declare a historic victory.

ADVICES

Not seeking advice can lead to disaster.

Asking for advice might also turn out poorly.

Receiving unsolicited advice

Can be an even greater problem.

Finally, accepting and following advice

Without having requested it

Can be the worst disaster of all.

RECIPE FOR A DISASTER

When you try to be too clever,

Attempting to outsmart nature,

And challenging a God who remains indifferent,

You gain no value for yourself or the world.

Instead, by embracing who you are,

You at least have a chance, not to outsmart,

But to be on equal footing with yourself.

And that is worth striving for.

ETERNAL YOUTH IN MEMORY

When there is no loneliness,
Loneliness feels lonely,
Murmuring tirelessly the forgotten song.
Don't grow old, even as time passes,
Even when oblivion wraps you in its embrace.

Stay young, at least in your memories,
When every moment is squeezed into one.
As time flows, let the heart remember
The joy, the laughter, and the dreams,
For in these echoes lies eternal youth.

LIFE IS POETRY

Good poets are good copy editors.

AMATEURS

There is no better or worse;
It's all a matter of taste.

BANANAS

Brother liked bananas.
If there were fifteen bananas,
And he was alone,
He would still leave two for us.

DOGS AND MEN

When a dog makes a friend,
It's a certainty.
When a man makes a friend,
It's unpredictable.

SAYING GOODBYE

To say or not to say more,

That is the question.

As I reflect now,

I've shared all I needed to express,

And have nothing more to add,

Except to say goodbye.

ABOUT THE AUTHOR

Dejan Stojanović (1959) was born in Peć, Kosovo (formerly part of Serbia, Yugoslavia). Although he received a legal education, he has never practiced law. Instead, he became a journalist and foreign correspondent in the early 1990s; however, he is primarily a poet, essayist, philosopher, and businessman.

He has published the following poetry collections:

Circling (Krugovanje), Narodna knjiga—Alfa, Belgrade, published in three editions: 1993, 1998, and 2000.
The Sun Watches Itself (Sunce sebe gleda), NIP Književna reč, Belgrade, 1999.
The Sign and Its Children (Znak i njegova deca), Prosveta, Belgrade, 2000.
The Creator (Tvoritelj), Narodna knjiga, Belgrade, 2000.
The Shape (Oblik), Gramatik, Podgorica, 2000.
The Dance of Time (Ples vremena), Konras, Belgrade, 2007.

Pentalogy: *The World in Nowherness (Svet u nigdini),* Udruženje književnika Srbije, Belgrade, 2017:
(1) *Ozar (Ozar),*
(2) *The World and God (Svet i Bog),*
(3) *The World in Nowhereness (Svet u nigdini),*
(4) *The World and Humans (Svet i ljudi),*
(5) *The Home of Light (Dom svetlosti).*

The Hidden Light (Skrivena svetlost), Čigoja, Belgrade, 2018.
Primordial Spark (Iskra iskona), Albatros plus, Belgrade, 2021.
Centuries and Steps (Vekovi i koraci), Albatros plus, Belgrade, 2023.

Essays:
Creator and Creating (Stvaralac i stvaranje), Albatros plus, Belgrade, 2021.
The New Man and the New World (Novočovek i novosvet), Rad, Belgrade, 2022.

Anthology: *Selected Serbian Plays* (*Izabrane srpske drame*), USA, 2016.

A book of his selected interviews, *Conversations* (*Razgovori*), was published in 1999 by NIP Književna reč in Belgrade. The Serbian Heritage Foundation and the Association of Writers of Serbia for Intellectual Engagement awarded the book the Rastko Petrović Prize.

Collected Poems: 1978-2000 (Pentalogy 1), New Avenue Books, 2025 (Translation from Serbian).

Books written in English:

Philosophy: *Absolute,* New Avenue Books, USA, 2024.

Poetry Series: *The Embrace of Light and Darkness* (Pentalogy 3):
- *Dance of Sounds*, New Avenue Books, 2025
- *The Matter of Matter*, New Avenue Books, 2025
- *The Home of the World*, New Avenue Books, 2025
- *All Women in One*, New Avenue Books, 2025
- *The Light of the Mind*, New Avenue Books, 2025

He lived in Chicago, USA, from 1990 to 2014, and holds citizenship in both Serbia and the United States.

www.ingramcontent.com/pod-product-compliance
Lightning Source LLC
Chambersburg PA
CBHW031029030726
47497CB00004B/1071